WRANGLED FATE

BOOK ONE: BLACK CLAW RANCH

CECILIA LANE

A SHIFTING DESTINIES NOVEL

CONTENTS

Tansey Nichols blasted through the door of the bar with the fury of a woman intent on getting answers or committing murder, and promptly bounced off the enormous chest of a Vagabond enforcer.

The wolf shifter crossed his arms and stared cold eyes down at her. "Club meeting. Get gone."

Tansey glared right back. "I need to see Viho."

She tried to lean around the man, but he shifted to block her view of the rundown bar.

"Club meeting. Get gone," he repeated.

Anger clenched her teeth so tightly she thought they might crack. She'd been building up to this all morning and afternoon. No way would she be chased away so easily. "Viho. Now."

"Let her by, Bryce."

Viho Valdana, alpha and grand president what-the-fuck-ever of the Vagabonds, waved her into the bar. A bottle rested at his elbow and a barmaid perched on his knee.

He was attractive, she guessed, but not her type. Straight black hair hung to his shoulders and the time he spent on the back of a bike darkened his natural olive skin. He was big and fit like the rest of his men, but they didn't have his speed or the intense bad boy undercurrent that always radiated off him.

Tansey didn't have time for bad boys. She didn't have time for good ones, either. The only man that concerned her at that moment was her brother.

Straightening her shirt, Tansey shot Bryce—who rode in a motorcycle club and kept the name Bryce? —a smug look and stalked across the creaky wood floor.

The bar was exactly the sort of place she'd avoided her entire life. Low lights made it hard to see, though the shifter crowd didn't have that problem. Dust covered everywhere that wasn't regularly used. She didn't have an enhanced sense of smell, but she could still identify spilled beer left to air dry.

All the current patrons wore leather vests with Vagabond patches. All were shifters. They shot her carefully calculated glances made to say that she was noticed and deemed nothing more than an annoyance.

Tansey focused on her target settled in a booth where he could see everything. She slid across from him, dismissed the barmaid with a flick of her eyes, and met Viho's blank look. "We've been here three days. Do you have any news?"

There was no mistaking what she was after. Rye had been missing for a full month. The first week saw her worrying and calling his friends and coworkers, then poking around the police station in their tiny, Minnesota hometown.

A chance encounter outside the station brought her face to face with Viho. He wasn't scared to track down a new shifter because he was one himself. For a small, inconsequential finder's fee, he'd take on her case and find her brother.

Only Tansey wasn't stupid. She wasn't about to hand over her cash and hope for the best. She agreed to the weekly fees with the condition that Viho let her tag along.

She hadn't expected the journey to be a slow crawl with stops to drink and fuck in every shithole bar that caught their fancy. Nudging Viho along was like pulling teeth from an impossibly wiggly crocodile, especially when all he wanted to do was fondle the barmaid.

Viho gestured to the bar filled with his people drinking long before it was five-o'clock anywhere decent. "What do you think I'm doing now? I'm working for you as we speak."

And yep, those were his fingers dipping under the barmaid's skirt. Her head dropped back, her eyes slid closed, and a tiny sigh escaped her lips.

Gross, but Tansey wouldn't be put off by the public display of horniness.

She'd been around the wolf pack enough to know they liked fucking with her. Shaking their dicks around after a shift, catcalling, and staring her down like mad dogs were everyday occurrences to test her limits. She also knew not to back down. Backing down was weakness and made them want to attack.

"It looks like you're wasting away another day when we could be on the road and hunting for leads. I thought you were supposed to be a good tracker."

Viho's carefree attitude slipped for a brief second and a too-long stare. Then his knee jerked and he spilled the barmaid to her feet. His hand squeezed her ass and urged her forward. "Get us refills, will you, darlin'?"

The woman glared at Tansey as if it were entirely

her fault for the case of blue balls, and not the man who got her going merely as a ploy to drive someone off. Not that she was alone for long. Two wolves hopped off their barstools and followed in her wake.

"Dawn's a good girl," he said as if reading her mind. He watched Dawn's progression through the pack and around the bar. "She'll tease them till their dicks could cut diamonds, but she won't let them touch her. Unless I say. She'd let the whole damn pack take a turn and still come crawling back to me on hands and knees as long as I gave her what she wants."

Shifter blood. Vampires weren't the only supes that could share. Hell, they all could, as far as she knew. She'd never touched a drop herself, but the Vagabonds made good money for opening up a vein and letting humans ride the high of increased strength and libido.

For the millionth time, Tansey wanted to drop her head into her hands and scream. Her life really took a nosedive into an already impressive downward spiral about a thousand miles ago.

Rye never before made her worry. Even after she moved to the big city, he kept her updated on small-town happenings and news about their overworked mother. They'd been close since childhood. Rye wasn't the sort to pull a vanishing act.

But then, she never thought their father would walk out on the family. And when she started dating, she never thought she'd see each and every relationship end the same way.

Maybe it was her. A not-insignificant part of her raised the question late at night, while she showered, and anytime her mind drifted. That miserable voice rang louder every day she didn't hear from her brother. She was rotten inside and eventually everyone had to get away from the smell.

"Do you have anything for me, or not?" Tansey asked testily. She didn't want to scent the air with her unease. She'd already pushed Viho once.

"My pretty flower, you really need to learn to multitask." Viho grinned around the bottle of beer and pointed a finger at her. "I, and a few close friends, know just how to teach you."

Gag. She hated being called a flower. And double gag for his innuendo.

She didn't respond, though. That would prove he'd gotten under her skin, and he would keep at her like a dog with a bone.

Finding Rye was the goal. No one else would take the case. Viho was her only option.

Silence stretched between them until Viho grew tired of the game. "This ain't the only joint Dawn tends. Couple of other folks she works with might have seen your brother with a local recently. Unless I'm very wrong, this man holds the key to finding your brother."

Blood pounded in Tansey's ears. She couldn't believe Viho's words. Sightings never materialized into anything more than a path to the next town. Bits of Rye's scent didn't lead anywhere. Now, though, she knew where to find him.

"Where? Who?"

"Don't go doing anything stupid. You don't know this place like I do. A little human like you will get eaten up in seconds."

"The name, Viho," she demanded.

"I'd hate to see my pretty flower crushed. These are dangerous people capable of horrible things. No, we'll all be needed and we're not at our full strength right now."

She rolled her eyes. Meaning, they weren't done getting loaded, sleeping it off, then doing it all over again. "I'm going. What difference does it make to you?"

"The difference to me is you haven't paid up for the week."

Tansey expected that. She dug into her back pocket and slapped the wad of bills on the table between them. Her fingers still hurt from scrubbing dishes at a little diner connected to her shitty motel. Work was work and money didn't last forever, especially on the road. "I'm good for it. Give me the name."

Viho's flashed her a predatory grin. His hand closed over the cash and dragged it toward him slowly. "On the other side of these mountains, in a little place called Bearden, you'll find a man named Ethan Ashford."

Viho said more, but Tansey had already shoved to her feet and made a break for the door. Howls followed her outside to her tiny little junker parked next to a long line of motorcycles.

Bearden was a shifter enclave. *The* shifter enclave. And this Ethan would be made to tell what happened to Rye.

CHAPTER 2

E than Ashford crouched at the side of the cow and pressed a hand to her neck. Still warm. That gave him comfort. Whoever kept killing his cattle wasn't in his clan. He wouldn't need to put any of his men down today. Thank fuck.

That this one had been cut from the herd and sent running through the night filled him with fury almost as much as the wasteful death. She'd been the first to get heavy with a calf out of the entire enclave. If she'd dropped early, she'd have brought him some desperately needed prize money as winner of the Calving Celebration.

Instead, she'd been bled and left entirely alone. Whatever killed her hadn't even taken a nibble. At least the others made a fine meal.

Three had been taken in the last month. The ranch ran at near zero profit already. Losing cattle only exacerbated his problems.

Which meant another year of working with Trent, the unbearable alpha of the lion pride on the next ranch over. Trent wasn't any good with humans, and Ethan didn't have extra horses. They'd been bullied into an arrangement where Trent loaned Ethan the horses and they split the profits from running trail rides for tourists curious to see how the shifter menaces lived.

Only with Becca, their bully, focused on her newborn cubs, Ethan had no one to run interference with Trent when the deal inevitably blew up as it had the past two years. The dead cattle and the vanishing prize money meant no extra money to invest in his own extra mounts.

His inner bear fed on his frustration and growled. Dammit. Holding his hand out to anyone was the last thing he wanted to do, but it was either that or let the ranch and clan shrivel into nothing. He'd rather die than give up on the place.

Black Claw Ranch was his birthright. He'd worked it from the time he could walk. His sweat and blood covered every inch of the land. Some years were better than others, but they were still *his*.

The bad went along with the good, and he wouldn't turn away from his responsibility.

Still didn't solve his current problem, though. Someone was killing his cattle and showed no signs of stopping.

At the snap of a branch, Ethan twisted and hauled up his rifle to point it at the threat. Even in an enclave full of apex predators, their natural kin made an appearance. With the press of human civilization on one side and being on the edge of the enclave territory, he saw more than most.

Nothing natural glared back at him in the golden eyes staring him down. The size of the wolf, too, gave the shifter away. The thick, black coat rose with its snarl. Head lowered and tail between its legs, the beast was making the threat known.

Ethan tried to catch the scent of the shifter. Downwind. Fuck. No telling who challenged him until he pushed closer. He bared his teeth and growled.

The wolf wasn't the first he'd seen. They lurked in the shadows, and always downwind. Too often, he only caught their scent long after they'd passed through his territory.

Watchers in the woods. Dead cattle. The oppressive air felt just like he remembered of the days before his father's war. Only then, the threat came from within.

The wolf took one step forward.

Ethan let his bear's growled warning enter the air. Together, man and beast, they laid claim to the territory.

The wolf stepped forward again.

Pushing for territory always carried a risk. Playing it safe meant caring for a clan in the space already carved out for them. Expanding, that could mean war. War and death went hand in hand.

Ethan prodded at the tiny studs in his brain. Each of his clan, they were there. Tied to him. Didn't matter how far they were apart, he could feel them. And if a life ended, the bond snapped back into him like a rubber band. The sting remained forever.

War was a risk. Too many snaps could destroy a man. He'd seen it happen when his father lost everyone.

The wolf stepped onto his land, killed his prize cow. That couldn't go unpunished.

But then the pack might hit back.

Ethan juggled the ideas. Safe, and being trampled. War, and death madness.

He aimed carefully. Just a brush of his finger against the trigger...

Horses crashed through the brush behind him, and loud voices jerked his attention to his clan riding hard.

Ethan swung his gaze back. The wolf was gone.

He wasn't sure if the clan quieted or pulled their horses to a stop first. Unease and anger swirled in their collective scent as they caught sight of the dead cow. They knew the cost added to the others lost.

"Fuck," Alex muttered.

The others added curses of their own.

Only Jesse, Ethan's second, stayed silent. He dipped the brim of his Stetson to hide his eyes.

Ethan shoved his rifle into the scabbard hanging from his saddle. His horse hitched up a hoof and gave a big sigh as he ran a hand down his splotched red and white neck.

He turned his attention back to the four men looking to him for guidance. "Don't you fuckers have fences to mend?"

"Thought you might need help tracking," Lorne answered quietly. "You left before breakfast."

"Lucky. You missed this one's walk of shame." Alex jerked a finger in Hunter's direction.

Hunter leaned on the saddle horn and grinned with zero shame. "Joyce wanted to get together—"

The group groaned.

CECILIA LANE

Ethan shook his head. "I'll order you not to see her again if that's what it takes. She's poison, man. Let her ruin someone else's life."

Hunter just shrugged and flashed another infuriating smile. "You're just saying that because you've never been in love."

Alex heeled his horse closer and whacked Hunter on the back of his head. "Neither have you, idiot. Nor have any of the other hundred guys she's been with."

A growl ripped out of Hunter and he flung himself out of the saddle and at Alex. They tumbled to the ground as their horses calmly stepped out of the way. The animals were used to it.

Hell, the true animals were the ones rolling around and throwing punches at one another.

They were a little wilder out on the ranch, and definitely not as tame as the shifters living in town. His bears needed to blow off extra steam from time to time. Like, every day. The regular brawls let them know where their place was in the pecking order. That structure helped when they were otherwise out of their minds.

Ethan scrubbed a hand through his hair. All those faces looking at him needed something. Food on the table, money in their wallets, a place to sleep. They were his clan, and he couldn't let them down.

His sister needed him, too. The happiest day of his life had been the day Colette received her acceptance letter to her top choice university. Oh, he'd calculated the cost of room and board and tuition on the fly and barely kept his wince in check, but nothing beat seeing the proud grin on her face.

He'd thrown everything into keeping the ranch running and making sure his sister had more opportunities than he had. No matter what he did, how hard he worked, it was all unraveling. Dead cows, broken fences, fucked up bears in his clan. Nothing was right and everything he brushed against rubbed him raw.

He was responsible for them, so no use crying about it. Only thing to do was keep waking up in the morning and stuff his feet into his boots.

Ethan stepped in at the first flash of claws. He didn't mind the fighting, but he didn't need them mauling one another and missing out on work.

"Enough." The word was quiet, but power infused the order. Alex and Hunter snapped backward like they'd been grabbed by their necks. Hunter let it roll right off him, but Alex glared.

Ethan met him stare for stare. Newest member of

the bunch and turned by a rogue, the hothead needed extra watching sometimes. The monster under his skin pushed and poked until he received a reminder of who was in charge.

Right then, though, the biggest fire was Hunter.

"Hunter, bail money is coming out of your paycheck next time you get busted fighting whoever Joyce fucks around with behind your back. And there will be a next time, so don't go arguing about how she's a changed woman. Joyce comes crawling back as soon as you stop chasing, then turns her charms elsewhere when she has you snagged up again. I'm sick of it. I'm sure the cops are sick of dragging you to the station. Leave it be, buddy."

"For all our sake's," Lorne muttered.

"Fuck you," Hunter told the quiet man. He raised both hands in a one-fingered salute and grinned like a madman. "You're all just upset because I don't have to find some barfly to give me a pity fuck."

Jesse snorted. "Are we talking about the same girl?"

Ethan passed his hand over his face again. "Time to get to work, children. Alex, Hunter, mount up."

With more grumbling and elbows than necessary, the two men pulled themselves off the ground and hauled themselves back into the saddle. A sharp whistle cut the meaner comments and three of the four kicked their mounts toward the house.

Jesse stayed back. "You think it was the lion pride?"

Ethan shook his head. "Trent's an asshole, but he's an honest one. He wouldn't resort to this to win."

The entire celebration was a convoluted mess dating back to generations ago. As with all things in Bearden, one small activity to pass the time blew up into an entire ordeal. Any rancher wanting to compete had to go through a sniff test to ensure they didn't lie about mixing bulls and cows before the approved start date. Judges coordinated an exact release date and time for the randy bulls to meet their lucky ladies, and then nature took the reins. It was sheer ridiculousness, but tradition died hard and the prize money at the end was a nice incentive.

They'd just have to hope one of the other cows was further along than she looked.

Ethan swung into the saddle. Patches sidestepped in protest, lazy bastard. He clucked his tongue and tightened his knees to keep the horse steady, then gave Jesse his orders. "Split Hunter and Alex up for the day. We don't need them going at each other until they shift. Put Lorne and Alex on mending the fence. Maybe the labor will calm him down some. Maybe Lorne will talk some sense into him."

Jesse pulled a face. "No calming that one, I think."

"No calming him either if he bears out and won't shift again. He gets closer to snapping every time I have to order him back to his human skin." Ethan blew out a breath. Fucked up bears would be the death of him. "You take Hunter and watch the rest of the herd. I'm going to see if I can pick up any trails off the latest kill."

Jesse nodded. They'd been close since childhood and knew each other's moods practically before they sparked into being. "Careful out there. Wolves are watching."

Ethan wheeled his horse around and waved Jesse off.

Dead cows and watching wolves couldn't keep him down. He had a clan and a sister to care for, and a ranch to run. Failure wasn't in the cards.

CHAPTER 3

Tansey barely saw the tiny town of Bearden as she crawled toward the outskirts behind a lifted truck. She couldn't focus on the cute shops and budding greenery when a solid lead about her missing brother was so damned close. The unexpected curves in the road were the only thing that kept her from zipping around the big truck and speeding out of the mountains.

Ethan Ashford had been surprisingly easy to locate. The woman in the visitor's office had brushed back curly hair, frowned about trail riding season starting up early, and shoved an address toward Tansey when her twins started to fuss.

The truck in front of her finally turned off onto a muddy trail. The slow speed on the road was quickly abandoned for a revved engine and zoom into gunk. Tansey shook her head. Country fun didn't change, even over state lines.

Less than a mile later, her phone dinged with the notice to turn to her right. Too late, she flashed past a road and a sign. Grimacing at faulty technology, she looked for the next driveway to turn back around.

The twenty-minute delay made her antsy, but not as much as staring down the sign at the edge of the road. Words burned into wood named the place as Black Claw Ranch. Carved underneath in uneven lines—maybe by one of the shifters themselves— were three claw marks.

For a quick beat, she regretted coming on her own. She employed Viho precisely because he had an animal nature and claimed he could track down any shifter. He was the tough one.

Not that she couldn't hold her own, but they were, well, *shifters!* Strong and deadly, with fangs and claws and muscles she didn't possess. Even the name of the place described their natural weapons.

Maybe it a test of her conviction. She didn't know or care. She had her heart set on finding her brother, and Ethan Ashford held the key.

Tansey passed her fingers over the cold barrel of

the pistol jammed between the door and her seat. Bless the hateful little hearts of the gun store employees for carrying silver bullets so close to shifter territory. She personally didn't have anything against the supernatural community. Hell, her brother willingly got himself bit to become one! But she was a modern woman, and precaution had been socialized into her from a young age.

Her car bounced over the cattle grate and crawled up the dirt road, shaking with every bump and tire track and rock she hit. Even mostly out of the mountains, the landscape was more hill than flat sprawl of the Midwest.

Finally, she rounded a bend. A big house sat on the top of a hill. Two stories, with at least two over-hanging decks she could see, and a spacious porch with wooden columns, it looked like an oversized, luxurious log cabin.

More than enough room to hide her brother.

A little further off was another big, unpainted building with wide double doors thrown open. A handful of horses grazed inside a fenced area. Two lifted their heads and whickered when Tansey pulled to a stop next to a silver pickup and stepped out of her much older vehicle.

The first thing she noticed was the air. The fresh

crispness of early spring mingled with the strong scent of honest work. Horses, cows, and hay overlapped in a pleasant way. Much better than the musty scent of stale beer and leather she'd grown to expect whenever the Vagabonds stopped at a bar. Infinitely more enjoyable than the harsh odor of trash and gas that built up in a city.

The second thing she noticed was a hunk of a man easily hauling a bale of hay out of the barn and tossing it into the open back of a truck.

Hello, cowboy.

If she'd been a cartoon character, her tongue would have rolled out of her mouth and onto the ground like a carpet.

Dark jeans clung to his legs, with worn spots on the insides of his thighs, his knees, and his ass. Sweat glistened on his skin, which was a delicious tan that just couldn't be replicated by any salon bed. A smattering of tattoos covered his shoulders and upper back in a tasteful display that was just the right amount of badass and take-him-home-to-mother. All six feet and several inches were packed with hard muscle. She tried counting the stacks of his abs and forgot what number came after six.

Then he caught sight of her, and she thought she'd swoon.

His eyes were shaded by his cowboy hat, but she didn't miss the strong jaw covered in stubble. One half of his mouth hitched up in a sexy smirk. "Can I help you?"

Yep, she was going to melt into a puddle. Of course he had a deep voice perfectly designed for dirty murmurings in the middle of the night.

"I'm looking for Ethan Ashford."

His eyes roved down her body and his smile widened when he reached her face again. "I'm Ethan. You are...?"

This was it. She just needed to ignore the smile that launched a thousand dirty thoughts. Too bad the impossibly sexy man was the one who last saw Rye, and maybe still had him locked up somewhere.

She'd tried to imagine how the conversation would go when she found Rye again, and then what she would say to anyone who had anything to do with his disappearance. Nothing ever jumped out as the right words. Too many variables dropped in and out of place to form a game plan.

"I'm Tansey. Tansey Nichols," she said, with an emphasis on her last name. Ethan didn't show any reaction, so she went on. "I was told you might know what happened to my brother."

Rye was the goal, not ogling some handsome

cowboy and wishing to jump his bones. What were those obnoxious window clings she'd seen on trucks? *Save a horse, ride a cowboy.*

Another time, maybe. If she drank away her inhibitions. A man looking like that had no use for someone plain like herself. He could have the pick of the tourists, and the locals, too.

His eyebrows shot together and he adjusted his hat. "Come again?"

"My brother. Someone saw him with you. He's been missing for a month." She swallowed her words and her desperation.

"Look, lady. Tansey. I don't know who you're talking about—"

"Rylan Nichols, goes by Rye."

"Can't help you. Never met a Rye or a Rylan." He cleared his throat. "Sorry he's disappeared on you."

"He didn't disappear. He's missing. One would be his fault, the other is on someone else," she snapped.

Ethan blew out a long breath and pressed his lips together in a hard line. "Okay," he said in a patient tone. "Why do you think I know your brother?"

They were going around in circles. That didn't win Ethan any points, and just made him look guilty. "The man I hired to track Rye down told me," she answered in what she called her customer service voice. It was used solely for unreasonable people. "He said Rye met with you, and no one has seen him since. So I'm asking you again, where is my brother?"

"Oh yeah? And who would that man be?"

"I hired Viho Valdana to track Rye—"

"The Valdana pack?" His whistle plummeted with all her hope. "Fuckin' A, woman. Do you have any idea the trouble you're in?"

"I know they tracked him here—to you. I know you're hiding something. Tell me what happened to Rye." She wasn't about to let him twist her into a different conversation.

"And you trust them? How did a pretty girl like you get tied up with them anyway?" His expression darkened and a muscle jumped along his jaw. "You one of them wolf hounds?"

The derision in his voice left no doubt what he meant. Tansey bristled. "No," she spat. "I'm not sleeping with any of them. Not that it's any of your concern. They're helping me find my brother—"

"You said that already. Maybe he doesn't want to be found."

"How would you know? Did he tell you that himself?"

Ethan growled, and she hated how much she

liked the noise. She could almost imagine feeling it vibrate through her.

"Don't know him, never met him. Tell Viho to stay the fuck off my land when you go crawling back to him. Have a nice life, Miss Nichols."

His words washed away the brief flush of desire. Tansey resisted the urge to stomp her foot. She just wanted to go back to the way things were a month ago. She knew where Rye was, knew what she'd be doing in the morning, knew where she'd go to bed at night. It wasn't a glamorous life, but it was an easy one.

The safe familiarity had been replaced by Viho's lack of respect, potentially no loyalty or trust from her brother, and a mouthy cowboy shredding all her plans to set her world right again.

With a final tip of his hat that felt like a slap in the face, Ethan turned back toward the barn.

A month of zero leads, worry, and frustration boiled over into hazy anger. He did not get to walk away from her!

Tansey reached inside the door of her car and then took careful aim. Her thumb brushed back the hammer.

"You're going to tell me where Rye is. Now."

CHAPTER 4

E than ignored the growling protest from his bear. The spitfire behind him had the beast quiet as she asked her questions, then raging when Ethan got sick of the accusations. Any other time or place, and he'd have bought her a drink and tumbled her against the nearest flat surface to make her come again and again. Something told him she'd be fun company for a night.

Accusing him of what, kidnapping? Murder? That killed his mood, if not his bear's. And she was tied up with Viho Valdana. Fucking asshole, and his Vagabonds were no better. That woman would be chewed up and spat out in no time at all.

Ethan couldn't ignore the cock of a gun.

The sound was loud over the beat of her heart

and the steps of the horses in the paddock. The sharp crack stretched into eternity and echoed the word *danger* back to him.

Ethan froze. He lifted his hands slowly into the air. He eased his foot to the side and twisted his body to find Tansey pointing a tiny pistol straight at his head.

"Put the gun down and we'll talk," he said in a calm, soothing voice.

She settled further into her stance. Her arms didn't waver. "How about we talk now? Where is my brother?"

"You're going to get someone hurt. Do you even know how to shoot that thing?"

Tansey's eyes narrowed. It was the only warning he had before she jerked the gun to the side and fired off a round two inches from his boot.

"Motherfucker," Ethan growled. His ears rang painfully, and he expected his bear to try ripping out of his skin. He braced himself against the threat, and when it never materialized, he sprang into action.

Tansey opened her mouth—no doubt to make more demands—then screeched as he grabbed hold of a wrist. A quick step put him behind her and his arm locked her against him.

His eyes nearly rolled to the back of his head as

her body molded to his. How the fuck did she fit perfectly against him? She smelled like honey and freshly baked pie. Even her long, brown hair was softer than silk. All his blood rushed straight to his dick while his skin felt tight and on fire.

Mine.

His thought, his bear's sending, didn't matter. Tansey Nichols was right where she belonged.

First, that gun had to go.

Ethan snapped into motion and pried her fingers from around the handle. He whipped it away from them both, pushed the release button, and let the magazine fall to the ground.

Better that than blowing out both their eardrums as he fired off all the rounds. One shot would have the clan running to check in with him. Multiples would have them running and ready to tear into anyone unfamiliar. He couldn't let them maul Tansey in a fit of misplaced protection. She might have shot at him, but he didn't want her dead.

He had to respect the toughness required to storm onto someone else's property and whip out a weapon. She wasn't the sort of woman to back down from a hangnail, much less the challenges of ranch life.

His bear paced in the back of his head, watching

her. No ounce of wariness existed in the beast. He was curious and impressed and wanted to keep her.

Ethan nearly stumbled. Neither his thoughts nor his bear's were the thinking of a sane man or beast. Tansey was a danger.

In danger.

Fuck.

Her elbow jabbed him in the side and brought him crashing back into honey-scented and soft-skinned reality. Her round ass rubbed against his dick as she struggled. Double fuck. She was going to think the worst of him if she felt his growing erection.

"Now that you won't accidentally kill me, I'm going to let you go. Then we're going to talk this out like civilized folk. Got it?"

She tried to free herself again, but no amount of wiggling would get her out of his grip. One arm locked around her chest and the other, after he stuffed her pistol into the waist of his jeans, clamped down around her hips.

Smelling strongly of frustrated anger and delicious honey, Tansey nodded.

Reluctantly, he let her loose. She snarled as ferociously as any shifter and scrambled to get clear of his reach. His bear rumbled in amusement. She'd been caught before, and the beast couldn't wait to give chase again.

Ethan shoved the creature to the far corner of his mind and walled him off for good measure. Tansey wasn't theirs, wasn't to be touched, and certainly wasn't to be chased. If he wanted to get laid, there were far easier options than a woman spitting mad and prepared to claw out his eyes.

Her jaw set in a stubborn line and she crossed her arms over her chest. "So, talk."

"Oh, no," he chuckled. "You shot at me. You get to answer my questions now."

Whiskey-colored eyes narrowed. "Ask away. I'm an open book," she gritted out.

"For starters, who the fuck said they saw me with your brother?"

"Why, so you know who to make disappear next?"

Ethan had to wipe the smile off his face. Damn, she was mouthy. He had nearly a foot on her and an animal under his skin, but she didn't back down.

She did just shoot at him, though. And on information given to her by his chief rival.

"Tansey," he said sharply. He liked how her name tasted on his lips. "Tell me what happened. How did you get my name?"

"Viho stopped three days ago at a bar to the west. One of the girls that works there heard it from someone else at another bar that Rye came through here, and you were the last person seen with him."

"Did you stop to think, 'gee, maybe these men willing to send me on a murder mission might, themselves, be capable of killing?' There's a reason they're not welcome in the enclave and it ain't because they're overzealous with the bar tabs."

"That doesn't make any sense. If they wanted you dead, why would they send me? Not like it was a challenge to disarm me."

The last was a mutter under her breath and accompanied by a flick of her eyes. Annoyance, yes, and something else. A little bit of heat, maybe.

"You don't know a thing about that pack, do you? Nothing is so simple with them. They like to play with their prey before making a move. Probably what they're doing with you." His bear shoved forward and readied for the attack. He wanted wolf blood, and not because of their incursions onto Black Claw territory. Viho's pack was a threat to Tansey.

"Look," she drew a shuddering breath. "This was the one and only lead I've had since Rye went missing. I need to know what happened to him. He's never disappeared like this before, and his house was a mess. Something happened, and the only one willing to listen was Viho."

A pang of pity tightened his chest. He understood her need to know where her brother ended up, and how. He'd jump through fire if the same thing happened to Colette.

Against his better judgment, he took a step closer. She flinched, so he held out his hand like he did when a horse shied away from him. "I don't know what happened to him. I don't know him. But if it makes you feel any better, I'll let you look through our books. We haven't run any trail rides since the season ended last year, so maybe that'll be proof he hasn't shown up here."

It was all he could offer.

It allowed him a few more minutes inhaling her sweet scent before they parted ways forever.

Heat flashed through him at the possibilities. He'd never had such a strong reaction to a female, human or otherwise. Love wasn't in the cards for him. He didn't wear his heart on his sleeve.

That flash fire left his objections in ash and wanted him to spill every thought to the woman.

Fuck that.

She was wrapped up with Viho, and he had a

ranch to run. Even if he wanted a mate—which he didn't—she wasn't the one for him.

His bear rampaged through his mind.

The sharp crack of a second gunshot ripped the hat off his head.

Ethan threw himself at Tansey, cradling the back of her head with his hand as they went down. The hard ache in his palm saved her a bump on the head. He covered her body with his to protect her from any other shots.

"Are you okay?" he asked her.

Silence blanketed the ranch.

CHAPTER 5

For the second time that day, Tansey found herself wrapped up in strong arms. Ethan's hard chest pressed into her own softer frame and squeezed the air from her lungs.

"Get off me," she wheezed, and shoved at him vainly.

"Are you hurt?" he demanded again.

He propped himself up on his elbows and stared down at her. Even without all his weight, Tansey found it hard to breathe. The position was far too close to the dirty images she'd had at first sight.

Blue. That was the color of his eyes hidden under his hat. The color brightened the longer she stayed quiet, churning into an eerily beautiful silver.

Tansey swallowed hard. It was the adrenaline

talking. Nerves. They'd been shot at, for goodness sake. How had he kept it so together when she shot at his boots? "No. Nothing hit me."

He nodded once. "In the house, then. Now!"

Ethan's order fell on deaf ears, but she couldn't ignore the firm grip on her elbows hauling her to her feet. He shoved her forward and rushed her toward the big house. There was no time to question him. She doubted he'd listen. He still hovered right on her heels, shielding her from any potential harm.

Almost as soon as they tumbled through the door, he cocked his head. "Backup is coming."

She had no idea what that meant until she heard the thundering steps of boots hitting the ground. The men—shifters—seemed to materialize from every direction. Four, total, all on foot and looking ready for a fight, thundered up the steps or threw themselves over the porch railing and through the door.

"What the fuck happened?" one newcomer demanded.

Tansey was ushered further into the home. The hair on her arms raised as the air jumped with unseen electricity. The open space of a huge living room shrank with the size of the men crowding around her and Ethan.

Stupid. So stupid. They'd no doubt heard her gunshot and came running. How close had she come to death?

Rye was still out there. Somewhere. She needed to talk her way out of this mess and keep her blood inside her body where it belonged. Who else would look for her brother if she died?

"Who took a shot at you?" one with shoulder-length black hair asked.

The one with dark curls glared at her. "Two shots. Was it this one?"

Ethan held up a hand before any more questions could be fired off. "Jesse, Hunter, I want you to run the perimeter to the east. Lorne, Alex, check the herd, then start west." His eyes passed over her, glowing silver. "I need to talk to this one."

Her heart sank into her stomach. No one looked at her as they filed back outside.

Ethan cleared his throat. "Be careful," he called out to them in a gruff voice.

Two flicked him off, and a brief smile flashed across his face.

Then he turned to her, and the smile vanished.

Tansey held up her hands and backed away from him slowly. He stalked after her, eyes never leaving her face. One step, then another. She bumped into the back of a couch. She steadied herself against it, then skipped around to put it between her and the predator chasing his prey.

"Stop running."

The order whipped through her and froze her in her tracks. It was impossible to ignore the effect he had on her body. Danger radiated off him, and the thrill of it flooded instant desire through her all over again. Silver eyes trapped her in place.

Ethan's gaze dipped down her body. The silver had brightened when he returned to her face. With a growl, he paced away.

The loss of his nearness was like a plant shriveling in darkness. Her heart ached and her stomach sank.

Which pissed her off. He was nobody to her. One giant hunk, but nobody. Maybe involved with her brother's disappearance, definitely holding her captive, and oh shit, oh shit, *oh shit...*

Coming her way.

Ethan stopped with his toes an inch from her own. His thumb and forefinger pinched her chin and turned her face to him, his glowing silver eyes holding her still.

"You're going to tell me everything, understand?"

Her skin prickled with the pure power he

wielded, and she nodded. "What do you want to know?"

"Why are you here? How did you find your way to my ranch with the Valdana pack? What trouble have you brought to my clan?" Ethan let her loose and waved in the vague direction of the door.

There was more to it than simply attraction, she realized. Seeing him, however briefly, with his people triggered her worry for Rye and a deep jealousy. Those men came running at the first sound of danger. Ethan ordered them back into trouble, and wished them a safe return. She envied the loyalty displayed on both sides.

They'd probably have a grand time burying her body and getting drinks after.

Tansey took a step back. "I told you before. I'm just looking for my brother. Viho was the only one that would look for him."

"That's what I don't understand. You show up, then get shot at."

"Who says it was me they were aiming at? It was your hat that got hit," she countered.

Ethan grunted and sank into the nearest couch. He waved for her to take a seat. "Maybe. But why wait until now, and with you there?" He shook his head and stared into the empty air.

Tansey slid a look toward the door. Could she make it while he was distracted? The others were gone. She just needed to get into her car and gun it. She inched her foot to the side.

Ethan immediately jerked his focus back to her. "Sit," he growled. "You did shoot at me. You owe me some answers."

The air pressed all around her like she'd been dragged deep under the ocean. Her heart worked to beat, and her lungs struggled to inhale. She wanted to obey. Needed to.

Tansey stumbled back a step and fell into the chair behind her. The heaviness immediately lifted.

She quirked an eyebrow at Ethan. "What did you do to me?"

He didn't answer. "Why does your brother need tracking down? Couldn't you have just given him a call?"

"You think that wasn't the first thing I tried?" First thing, and a thousand times over since then. She thought she could dial his number in her sleep.

But that didn't answer Ethan's first question. When she dared glance at him, she found him staring back at her.

Blue had replaced the silver of his inner animal. She liked the color. It matched the sky outside.

She was already in the belly of the beast and she shot at him. Near him. She never intended to hit him, just jog his memory a little and make him see she meant business.

There wasn't any harm in giving him some information. Maybe it'd endear her to him and he'd let her go without any fuss. She could always leave out details if needed. She couldn't forget she was dealing with a potential murderer.

She wasn't even sure about that anymore. Someone had taken a shot at him, and he had thrown her down to protect her. He watched her with an intentness that stirred an awareness of him deep in her core.

God, she was going crazy. She wanted to throw her trust at anyone that might give her answers.

"Rye has always been a bit wild. Always in trouble. He was older than me, but he was always there. I remember the day he heard some older kids making fun of me for running off our dad. He got quiet, and told me to keep walking home. The next day, those kids were in the same spot as always, but they didn't say a word to me. Probably afraid he'd blacken their other eyes."

Those taunts were still loud and painful. The town was small, so of course the news of John

Nichols leaving his wife and kids spread like wildfire. He was a no-good asshole and a cheat, she later learned, but he was still her dad. And he left in the middle of the night without a goodbye.

Just like Rye.

Tansey twisted her fingers on her lap and stared at the floor. Maybe it was her. Maybe she drove everyone away. Rye probably got sick of her and just ghosted. Wouldn't be the first man in her life to drop her suddenly and without remorse. She guarded her heart like a dragon guarded its hoard because she was sick of letting others take whatever they wanted and leaving her dry.

"So you were close."

Ethan's words drew her out of her memories. She thought his eyes held a trace of pity.

She didn't want his pity, and she certainly didn't like the finality of his past tense *were*. She just wanted to find her brother.

"He's my best friend. He's always been my best friend. I know his habits, so I knew something was wrong when I couldn't reach him and he didn't call me. I went back home to check on him. The house was a mess, but there wasn't any sign of him. Everyone I talked to said his animal probably jacked up the place looking for a way outside."

Ethan sat up straighter. "He's a shifter?"

"A wolf, yes. Happened about a month before he went missing. He's been fascinated with you people since you were outed. I think he's always felt a little… weak? Not up to par with everyone else? He wanted to be more than a part-time bartender in a one-bar town."

She'd clawed her way out of there as soon as she finished high school. Something locked Rye to that place, and he wouldn't leave despite all her convincing. It became a joke over the years, him with his backwoods living and her with big city ideas. Sometimes she thought he waited for their father to return home.

"A wolf," Ethan repeated. His eyebrows drew together. "Do you know who bit him? Was it Viho's pack?"

"No. He never said." Tansey shook her head. "What do the Vagabonds have to do with his turning?"

"Wolves are… They are…" Ethan hesitated. "If this is a pack problem, if your brother was a Valdana, then maybe you're being used to get at him."

"But why send me out here and say you know what happened to him?"

"That's some rotten shit spanning back to my

father's time. Let's just say Viho wants my territory, and leave it at that."

He grimaced, and his fingers dug into the arms of the chair. Viho definitely had the man on edge.

Upset enough to abduct or murder one of Viho's pack? She wasn't so sure anymore.

Tansey tried to unknot the tangled threads uniting them both. She and Ethan were both connected to Viho. Rye, too, maybe. Rye was her reason for having anything to do with Viho.

She didn't like the idea of being jerked around for someone's plot. She also didn't like being kept in the dark with something that might concern her brother.

Tansey's jaw set in a hard line. "Let's not—"

Ethan cocked his head again, and cut her off with a raised hand.

Tansey quelled her wish to bite off the fingers that shushed her and listened closely. She thought Ethan tilted his head on purpose as a signal for her human senses. Sure enough, feet stomped up the porch and through the door.

Her eyes widened at the very naked man that stepped inside, and Tansey quickly looked elsewhere.

Ethan jumped to his feet. "Fucking hell, Hunter.

Put some damn clothes on," he growled, putting himself between them.

Hunter's grin didn't drop even as he found a pair of jeans by the door. "Jesse sent me back. We caught the scent of a Valdana wolf just past the huts. Fucker shifted and ran, but left his rifle behind."

CHAPTER 6

F *uck.*

Ethan's bear raged in his mind. He wanted to let fur fly, starting with the unmated male waving his dick around for his mate to see. He needed to bleed, learn his place, cower.

Ethan froze. His bear shoved forward in that moment of weakness and nearly brought him to his knees. A low, inhuman growl vibrated in his throat. He stopped the sudden shift by a fingernail.

Hunter stilled, too. He tilted his head to the side and exposed his neck.

The submissive move should have quieted his bear. It only made the beast angrier. No creature so weak deserved a mate like Tansey.

Tansey didn't notice the dangerous waters lapping at her ankles.

She slipped around him and planted her hands on her hips. Her glare took in both him and Hunter. "So, what? Viho sends me out here, then tries to kill you? What is the point of that?"

He didn't want a mate. Tansey was already a distraction he didn't need. She'd be a liability in any fight to come. Say he bonded the fragile human, and they had a few happy nights together. What happened when Viho killed her and that bond snapped back inside him?

Love and mates were as deadly an addiction as the one that took his father to the bottom of a bottle while his family and land fell apart around him.

He couldn't get involved. She wouldn't stick around. Viho was after her for some damned reason only a crazed wolf would know. She was being played. He didn't know what Viho's end goal was, but he was sure as fuck it'd end in blood.

Her blood.

His bear slashed at his insides. No one would hurt her. No one would get near.

Tansey's glare softened. "Ethan?" Concern swelled in her scent.

He should warn her away from shifters and send

her back to whatever town she called home. Would it even matter? She was so bullheaded stubborn, she'd probably turn right back around and try to shoot him again.

"You should stay here." The words were as equally big a surprise to him as to Tansey and Hunter. Fucking A, but he couldn't let Viho get to her. "I'll help you find your brother."

Or whatever was left of him after the wolves got hold of him.

"Thanks, but—"

"They shot at you—" he interrupted.

"Or at you, so—"

"So we're decided. Until we know who Viho is trying to kill, you'll stay here."

Her glower just made him grin. He liked how easy it was to rile her up. At least he wasn't in any danger of her shooting him at the moment.

He made a mental note to check the gun safe and add her little pistol to his personal collection.

"Why the hell would I do a thing like that?"

"Because Viho hates me, and he used you. I won't do that." Sweet fuck, he couldn't keep his mouth shut. He inhaled again. Honey filled his nose with no trace of bubbly magic. She wasn't fae, that was for sure. The hold she had on him was his own damn problem.

Confusion and amusement wafted off Hunter. His eyes bounced between Ethan and Tansey. He edged further into the house. "What's this about a brother?"

Ethan crossed his arms over his chest and silently dared Hunter to take another step closer. "Rye is a newly bit wolf and has been missing for a month. Tansey employed Viho to track him down."

Hunter's eyebrows tried to meld with his hairline. "Did you call the police? Maybe he's just chasing tail and doesn't want to come up for air."

Tansey's eyes narrowed. "He's not like that."

Her offended scent balled his fist. He slugged Hunter on the arm. "Have some respect, asshole. The man is missing."

Hunter rubbed his arm. "Fuck, sorry."

"Earn your forgiveness. Get dinner started. The others will be back by the time you're done," Ethan ordered.

It put more distance between him and Tansey, too. Ethan's bear approved. The only thing the beast wanted more was to make her meals himself and provide her a life of comfort. He settled with standing guard over her.

Tansey tracked Hunter through the open living room and into the kitchen. "I've been to the police," she sniffed. "The local cops told me they didn't have the ability to handle anything furry and to try animal control."

"Cute," Ethan said flatly.

She nodded with a grimace. "Right? So I dug around and found a small group of lynx that had registered, but they wouldn't get involved with any wolves. I didn't dare go to the Supernatural Enforcement Agency after all the bad coverage and attempted murder of prisoners. I didn't want to take the chance of drawing the wrong sort of attention to Rye.

"The tenth time I was escorted out of the police station for yelling at the chief, Viho was there. He caught up to me and offered his services. He's contacted people in your enclaves and tracked Rye. It's wiped out my savings, but we've gotten this far."

"Not very far," Ethan muttered. He scrubbed a hand over his face. Fucking Viho probably bled her dry and knew exactly where the brother was buried. "You say he's talked to our police?"

"First day we got near. Said they wouldn't divulge any information, so he started working the locals."

"That doesn't sound like Judah," Hunter called

from the kitchen.

His wasn't the sweetest clan. Or the meanest. They'd had enough run-ins with Bearden's police force to have a semi-decent relationship with the Chief. Blowing someone off definitely didn't sound like Judah.

His words surprised him again with their sudden existence. "Let me make a call. Maybe I can get you a meeting. He might be able to put you in contact with other enclaves. We'll find your brother."

At least he regained control of himself before he spoke the fateful 'I promise.' He hated going back on his word, and he doubted the man would be found so easily.

The hard set of her jaw softened and she slashed her eyes away from him. Getting hold of herself, he thought. She almost managed to keep hope out of her whiskey-brown gaze, but there was no hiding the overwhelming amount coloring her scent.

By the Broken, he didn't want to disappoint her.

He needed to get away before he did.

He padded further into the large living room to curb the temptation of pulling her into his arms for reassurance. She'd probably fight being so close, and he was wary of prolonging their contact. Just one favor, he promised himself. He'd set her on the path of real, genuine help, and be done with her before she pulled more trouble down around his head.

Bear clawing to get out, Ethan fished his phone out of his back pocket and dialed the number he knew by heart.

"Bearden Police Department non-emergency line. Please state your business."

"Hey, Jenny. Chief Hawkins in?"

"He's transporting a prisoner. Won't be back until the morning. Can someone else help?" Jenny sounded bored, and the quick rasp in the background gave away the filing of her nails.

"Can we get down for tomorrow, then?"

"Sure thing. Be here at eleven."

He ended the call, and updated Tansey.

"Tomorrow. Okay. I've waited this long. Another day won't be so bad." She wet her lips and turned her shoulders toward the door. "I should—"

"Stay," he interrupted. "We have extra space here."

He needed out of the house and away from her. Honey filled his nose and those gorgeous eyes were locked on his face. His blood pounded in his ears. His skin itched, his gums ached, and he wanted to give in to the constant roaring of his bear to keep her.

Ethan cleared his throat. "Let me show you to

your room. I have some work to finish up before dinner gets served."

The cold wash of responsibility did little to chill the fire in his veins. He couldn't sit around after all the excitement, and he needed a distraction from the mouth-watering temptation mere feet from him. With his blood pumping, all he wanted to do was reach for her and find some relief.

"Oh. Of course. I did sort of wreck your entire afternoon with some minor death threats."

"Wouldn't be a complete day without one of those," he joked back.

Sweet fuck. Soon she'd have him sitting by the fire with a pipe in his mouth as they chatted about the weather and neighbors.

One night. Then he could fob her off on Judah and get back to worrying about next month's bills and which of his bears he'd need to bail out of jail next.

Without another word, he started up the stairs. The creak of the wood told him she followed.

He led her through the upstairs loft and down the hall into the family wing. His sister's bedroom was mostly empty, but still hers. His old room had been abandoned long ago when he moved into the master suite on the ground floor. The two other rooms were meant for the clan if they ever needed the space.

The other side of the loft was an exact copy and meant for guests that hadn't existed in decades. He still made it a rule twice a year to shake the dust off the cloth-covered furniture and give the rooms a cleaning. His mother would have haunted him otherwise.

Ethan pushed open the door to a spare bedroom and flipped the switch inside. A soft glow spilled out into the hallway. "Here you go. You have any clothes or a bag or something in your car?"

She gestured at herself with a twist of her lips. "I just brought me. All my stuff is at a motel on the other side of the mountains."

"I'll have someone get them for you. That way you won't run into Viho." That someone would be him. Damn his mouth for running again.

Fur brushed against his awareness and he let his bear's sending push through. The scent of fur and blood paired with an image of Viho unsuccessfully crawling away from certain death. The scene and stench dissolved into Tansey's soft smile and scent of honey and gratitude.

He made his feet move over the snarling protests of his inner animal.

"Hey, Ethan?"

Her words wrapped down his spine and seized control of his muscles. He stopped in his tracks and turned back around. "Yeah?"

Light filtered through her hair and gave her a muted halo. Her throat worked twice before she asked her question. "What are you? Not a wolf, it sounds like."

"Bear. We're all bears here." Growling, snarling, clawing, wild bears with no place for a woman in their midst. Not even a tough one like Tansey.

A small smile raised her lips. "I've always liked bears."

His rebellious beast preened.

She was close enough to touch. His fingers twitched with the urge. He already knew how soft her skin felt under his rough palms. He'd gladly welcome her ample curves against him again.

Her pupils blew wide and her lips parted slightly. He bet she tasted every bit as intoxicating as her scent suggested.

Mine.

He stepped back. The spell she had on him broke when he dropped his gaze. "Make yourself at home."

Alpha, rancher, and man, Ethan fled the upstairs before he did anything stupid.

CHAPTER 7

Tansey woke before dawn. Muddled confusion fogged her brain as she snuggled further into warm blankets and a comfy mattress. She bolted straight up. Her motel room didn't have an ounce of luxury.

Her heart beat against her ribcage and she took several deep breaths before recognizing her surroundings. Sleep had been hard to find and must have stolen all her wits when she finally gave in to her exhaustion.

With the sour panic fading from the back of her tongue, Tansey lay back down and stared at the ceiling. She needed to prepare herself for the day ahead and the ridiculously built cowboy that set it into motion.

She couldn't pinpoint why she readily agreed to let Ethan help and house her. Something about him made her want to trust. Stupid, she knew, especially when the only man she'd ever fully trusted vanished into thin air.

But Ethan seemed so... honest. The quality was lost on Viho, who made every interaction feel like it was covered in slime.

Maybe it was sheer desperation. In the space of a couple minutes, Ethan had gotten her closer to answers than Viho had in a month. Where the hell had he been when Rye first went missing?

A door below slammed closed. Someone growled. The door opened and closed again, quieter. Loud footfalls and clinking of glasses gave away the men awake at the ungodly hour.

The silence broke with a grumpy line of questioning. "So we're just inviting anyone we want to stay the night? Did you two enjoy your little sleepover?"

The kitchen must have been directly under her room. She could hear every word they said, and most of it was about her.

"It's not like that," Ethan rumbled. "I'm just helping her find her brother."

"No seeing if she needed someone to warm her

bed? Pity." The snort of laughter cut off with a gurgle and a thump.

"It's coffee time, Alex. Have some respect for this sacred hour before you run your mouth," Jesse chided. At least she thought it was him. He'd hardly said a word during the solemn dinner the night before.

That had been an awkward affair. The bear clan had gathered around a large table. Everyone's eyes darted between their plates, her, and Ethan. Except the man himself. He didn't once look up from his meal. After shoveling food down their gullets like they were in a speed-eating contest, they all scattered. Ethan remained long enough to throw the dishes in the dishwasher, then retreated to his corner of the house.

Well. She wasn't one to make herself scarce, especially when they gossiped about her.

Tansey rolled out of bed and tugged on a fresh pair of jeans. When Ethan rapped his knuckles on her door well past sunset, he had her bag slung over his shoulder. He'd also turned on his heels and charged back downstairs as soon as her fingers brushed against his and looped around the handle.

She was grateful for the help, but she'd be glad to

trade the ranch for anywhere she didn't feel like an unwelcome intruder.

The bedroom door didn't make a sound when she threw it open. She retraced her steps down the hallway and into the loft overlooking the open floor plan below.

No one spoke. Everyone studied the contents of their steaming mugs.

"Good morning," she said cheerfully. The false note in her tone grated even her nerves. More than one man's lips tightened in a small frown.

The quiet one—Lorne. He said the least of them all. She thought he grunted once at dinner, but couldn't rule it out as clearing his throat—tipped his hat and slid out the back door. Alex and Hunter shot sly glances at Ethan before following just as quickly.

Tansey frowned after the three. She tried to take a sniff of herself. Nothing wrong there. Even a cupped hand over her mouth didn't give her anything than normal morning breath. Coffee would cover that until she could brush.

Probably her fault. She drove people off in the best of times. Of course they wouldn't extend her any courtesy. Their loyalty was with Ethan. The welcome wagon lost its wheels right around the time she pointed a pistol at the man.

Well, she'd been commanded to stay. If they had a problem, they could take it up with their boss.

Tansey crossed the threshold from living room into the kitchen. The no-mans-land was clearly marked by a single step into enemy territory.

Her skin prickled with an unfamiliar energy. Even the air felt heavier, like it had before when she thought she'd drown right out in the open. She ignored it as best as possible, and made her way to the black gold in the pot between Ethan and Jesse.

"'Scuse me," she muttered as she reached for the handle.

Her arm brushed against Ethan. Instantly, heat flooded her veins and rapidly spread through her entire body. Even her toes wanted to curl.

Shocked, she jerked her eyes to the side and right at his unmoving chest. Up and up, over his solid chest and wide shoulders, until she peeked under the brim of his hat. Impossibly bright silver eyes stared back at her.

Right. Shifter things. She knew better than to get near any of the Vagabonds after a fight or deep into a night of drinking. She probably triggered some instinct to hunt fresh meat with her appearance first thing in the morning. Not wanting to be on the menu, she yanked her arm away from Ethan and shuffled to the large island floating in the center of the kitchen.

And promptly realized she had no mug.

Balls.

Ethan, eyes still glowing, pulled one from the cabinet behind him and set it down with a loud thud that had her wondering how it didn't crack.

The dark side of dawn wasn't her favorite time of the day either, but she wasn't throwing a damn fit. Not that she was in any position. He held the cards and the means to contact the Bearden police about her brother. She could deal with a little morning unpleasantness if it got her answers.

Tansey continued to fix her liquid fuel in utter silence. Her first sip didn't disappoint, and almost made up for the awkwardness still in the air. Not wanting to face the stony faces of the remaining shifters, she twisted in her seat and turned her attention to the home. She'd been too keyed up the previous night to give it a decent inspection.

Just past the front door were the stairs that curved upward with a landing between floors. The railing ended with the smooth carvings of bear heads on either side.

A huge stone fireplace dominated one wall. Comfortable, if old, sofas and chairs clustered around to give the feeling of privacy. A big bookshelf leaned against another wall, with large DVD collection on one side and plenty of books on the other.

It was the kitchen that snagged her undivided attention. Exposed beams ran from one end of the room to the other. The fridge looked newer than the giant oven by about ten years, but even the older fixtures appeared carefully cleaned and maintained.

It was exactly the sort of kitchen she hoped to run one day. A very, very distant one day, now that her meager savings had been handed over to Viho. Her employment record was wrecked, which ruled loans out anytime soon. But she'd have her own bed-and-breakfast one day, and could have all the social interaction she needed with none of the commitment she failed at.

"Your range is huge. Hard to believe it's just for you five," she blurted without thinking.

Jesse spoke to his coffee. "Not always. This place used to serve up rooms full of guests."

"Used to? What happened?"

He inclined his head slightly before finally settling on an explanation. "There was a change in ownership."

"Check on the others, will you?" A nod to Jesse accompanied Ethan's obvious end of the conversation. They exchanged a long, complicated look before Jesse broke and shambled off after the others, leaving them alone.

A shiver worked down Tansey's spine. The air felt heavy again, and not entirely unpleasant.

"You're up early."

The gruff words were at odds with the charming smile he flashed her way. Even the bright silver of his eyes didn't feel as harsh as before. Ethan ran hot and cold, it seemed.

"Used to be used to it. I've worked breakfast shift for a diner and prepped for a bakery, so early mornings aren't unknown. Just haven't seen them in a while since Viho never woke before noon." Tansey took a big swig of her coffee to stop her babbling.

His eyes darkened with what she thought was anger or annoyance. His tone was all dark velvet for more contradictions. "Did you sleep well?"

"As much as could be expected," she said evenly. "And you?"

"Tossed and turned."

The thought of him stripped down to nothing popped into her mind. His impressive chest and stomach had already been imprinted in her brain. She didn't need much prompting to imagine a soft dusting of hair on thick thighs, or what he packed between them.

She dragged her eyes away from his face and down his body. She doubted he was a boxers or a briefs kind of man.

Ethan rumbled, and she jerked her gaze back to his face. Busted.

She escaped the scrutiny and her traitorous thoughts by sliding off her chair and wandering into the living room. Along the fireplace mantle were a few framed pictures: a black-and-white of the home being built, an older couple she assumed were his parents by their shared features, and a larger group she thought might have been a family reunion.

The only modern photo was of Ethan with his arm wrapped around the shoulder of a younger woman. Her hair was slightly lighter than Ethan's but their eyes were the same.

"My sister," he said at her side.

Tansey nearly jumped out of her skin. Time with Viho had given her experience with shifters, but it didn't kill her shock when they moved fast and without noise. "Where is she?" she covered.

Hat off, he looked more relaxed. Even his shoulder didn't seem so tense. And the smile he flashed her scorched her insides.

"Colette is away for her third year of college. It costs a damn fortune, but she's happy," he answered with obvious pride.

Something close to kinship unfurled inside her. With that one tidbit of knowledge, Ethan showed himself to care just as much as she cared about Rye. He could play at being a tough, macho cowboy all he wanted, but his sister proved he had a gooey center. It was endearing.

At least she thought so until he spun on his heels and strode through the living room like his jeans were on fire. He slammed his hat down on his head and gritted out, "Have a nice morning, Miss Nichols."

Tansey gaped at him for a quick second, then she shot through the home just as he wrenched open the door. "Wait!" she yelled. "What about helping? Don't we have an appointment?"

He had a sister. He had to know how important it was to find Rye.

Ethan rounded on her. "Yes, I'm going to help. Yes, we have an appointment. It's hours away from now and I have a ranch to tend. The world doesn't stop turning just because you blew into my life."

"I never said that it did," she snapped back.

"Just—" His growl cut off his words. "Don't

wander off, okay?" The deep gravel of his voice matched the brightness of his eyes. Blue and silver swirled together.

"Why? Don't want any witnesses if I go missing like Rye?"

His strong jaw tightened and he adjusted the brim of his cowboy hat. She thought it was an excuse to delay his words. Or maybe he was swallowing all the curses he had for daring to question him.

"The lion pride on our border doesn't care for humans. You're liable to get hurt if you head out there. So do me a favor and stay put."

She didn't catch the words under his breath, but she could only assume they were impolite. "They don't like humans? That's despicable. Speciesist, even. I don't have anything against shifters, why would they have anything against me?"

Ethan's cold blue eyes locked on her face. "Because humans murdered Trent's parents in front of him. I need you to stay alive."

Tansey blinked. In that half second of shock, Ethan disappeared through the door.

Frustration built in her chest. She'd deluded herself that he actually cared, it seemed. Fucking awesome. A-plus reading of people, as always.

He'd protected her with his own body as a shield

and convinced her to stay, but that brief flash of inclusion was wrong. She couldn't hope for it to last with Ethan or his clan. She was a means to an end, a connection to the Vagabonds, and he didn't help her out of the kindness of his heart.

There was no counting on a man like that. The moment she became too inconvenient, he'd drop all pretense of helping her. No, better to forget his panty-melting smiles and gather any information she could before then.

Rye's life might depend on it.

CHAPTER 8

Ethan's bear roared. Sharp claws pierced his chest. His gums ached with descending fangs and his fingers hurt with the push of claws. The beast wanted out and didn't give a shit if Ethan objected.

Not a single sending in the world could force him back into his home. Her scent already coated everything and drove him crazy. He'd hardly slept, fighting his other half to keep from barging into her room and crawling into her bed. Then seeing her, hair tangled and bags under her eyes, drove another spike into his heart.

Dammit. She was not destined to be his mate, she was only somewhat his problem, and he had shit to do. People depended on him keeping steady. If he lost control, the tenuous grasp his clan had on themselves would snap. Colette wouldn't finish school. His herd would go unchecked and the ranch would be lost.

He didn't have time for the frustrated smelling woman he left behind or the rabid animal lashing out at his insides.

Ethan drew in a shaky breath and pried back control from his inner animal. Another deep inhale saw the tips of claws retreat back into fingernails. A third breath calmed his heart enough to hear over the pounding.

Cattle mooed near the barn. Too many to be anything but panic.

He strode straight for the open doors and found the others pulling out tack and readying their horses. "Tell me," he ordered.

"There's a break in the fence. A rough count shows five head are missing," Jesse said with a frown. There was more, and he didn't want to say.

"What else?" Ethan demanded.

Power whipped out of him. The others froze in their tracks and shot him dirty looks. Anger built in their scents, and confusion, too.

Fuck. He didn't mean to add a weight of dominance to the words. Tansey had him messed up.

Jesse answered as soon as the air cleared. "Wolf scents."

Of course. Of-fucking-course. Viho didn't succeed with his plan yesterday. He had to keep trying. Which meant the danger to Tansey was even more real.

He didn't know which way to turn. He wanted to protect the woman with every fiber of his being. He could stay and guard her in the house. He could track the wolves that hunted on his territory. Both options sounded fantastic to his bear. One would keep them in close proximity, the other would prove their fierceness.

He eyed the four men who looked to him for a livelihood. He'd be better out on the trail than repairing a fence and twiddling his thumbs waiting for a glimpse of Tansey through the curtains.

"Hunter, Lorne, get on fixing the fence. Until we know the wolves aren't around, I want you guarding the rest of the herd." He went to the tack room and pulled out his saddle. Patches hung his head over the stall and nickered as he swung open the door. Ethan leaned out of the stall. "And make sure our guest doesn't leave the house. No need to get her into more trouble. The rest of us will help find the missing head, or the wolves, whichever comes first."

There was only minor grumbling as the groups fell in line. The two being left behind stuffed thick gloves into their pockets. Hunter went to pull his truck around. They were throwing wire cutters and wire into the bed when Ethan finished brushing down and saddling Patches.

Alex and Jesse were already mounted up by the time he led the horse out of the barn. The first rays of light colored the sky as he slid his rifle into its place on his saddle and climbed up.

"Let's go."

Jesse heeled his horse forward, and Ethan followed with Alex right beside him.

It didn't take long to find the break in the fence. One post hung tangled in barbed wire, but the tension still meant most of the fence remained propped up.

No wonder only a handful of cattle were missing. They would have needed to be driven to jump over.

The stench of fur was proof of that. Paths crossed over one another so thickly, he could practically see the wolves driving each cow. They weren't after wholesale destruction. This was a game to them.

"I want someone watching the herd at all hours. We'll rotate until we know this won't happen again." More work, but they had to see it coming. He tried to spin it to himself as an early start to the calving season. Someone watched constantly then.

That was for new life. This was for more death.

Ethan growled and spurred Patches into a quick trot to follow the odor of the trespassers.

The scents were as strong an indicator as the dirt churned by hooves. Large paw prints crossed the loose track, showing the wolves nipping at the heels of the cattle. Each one compounded the fury rolling through his other half.

The wolves had come onto his territory, stolen his beasts, and threatened his mate. The bear wanted blood.

Ethan didn't have the energy to correct his raging animal. It took all his control to keep to his human shape.

They'd ridden through the foothills about an hour when the sharp tang of metal mixed with the other scents he tracked. He heeled Patches faster up one hill and pulled to a stop. Alex and Jesse drew up next to him and growled at the sight below them.

Earth had been torn up as the cow tried to dodge her attackers. She was dead. The kill was as clean as the other from two days ago. Throat torn out, left alone to bleed, with not a single bite taken.

Ethan squinted at the cow. The timeline was

fuzzy. Tansey said the pack had only arrived three days before she showed up on his land. The last cow was cut from the herd and killed the day prior to that. But there had been wolves watching him for weeks, and other cows taken, too.

Waiting on Viho, maybe. Because he was stringing along another mark, or because he purposefully drove Tansey toward Black Claw from the beginning?

Viho had it in for him, without a doubt. Ethan didn't understand the purpose of throwing the fragile human his way. Was he supposed to kill her, and see Viho rise up as some wronged creature? Was she supposed to kill him, and make way for Viho in the vacuum left behind? But why the second shot that found its home in his hat?

Too many questions made his temples pound with the beginnings of a headache. Truth was, there was no sense in puzzling out the wolf's motives. He wanted to fuck shit up, and he'd succeeded. Ethan was distracted with fixing Viho's messes when he needed to focus on providing for his people.

"Mark the spot." He fixed his eyes on Jesse. "We'll dispose of the carcass once we know what happened to the others. No use doing extra work if they're dead, too."

The sun had climbed another hour while they zigzagged across his territory. The path carried them to the far edges along the border of another ranch.

Ethan's frown deepened when Alex turned in his saddle.

"Riders," Alex announced. His nostrils flared and his nose wrinkled with slight disgust. "Lions."

The last thing he needed was a run-in with Trent to turn a terrible day to absolute shit.

Hoping to avoid an unnecessary brawl, Ethan glanced to his men, then to the sun. "Ride ahead. Finish this up."

"So you can get back to your woman faster?" Alex sniped.

Jesse took the sting from the other man's words with a teasing grin of his own. "Now, Alex, don't mock him. He's only been looking over his shoulder every two minutes."

"Fuck you both. I need to turn back to take her to Judah." His dick twitched in anticipation of seeing her again. He wanted to replace death, fur, and dirt with her honeyed scent.

Alex grunted. "Only reason you're turning back now is because that little human caught your eye. There's more important business, alpha." His eyes flashed inhuman green as his voice dropped to pure gravel.

Ethan ground his teeth together. Alex had his reasons for being an utter asshole ninety percent of the time, but they couldn't sort it out right then. He should have known the man would be a mess with a woman in the house. His maddening comment that morning was just the beginning.

Trent and two others crested over a hill. They pulled to a stop not far from the fence line. "What's this about a human?"

Ethan glared at Jesse and Alex. Motherfuckers.

He leaned against the saddle horn and pushed the brim of his hat up with one finger. "Got a girl stashed at my place. She won't be a bother."

"Human girl? She ain't one of us." Trent leaned to the side and spat.

Ethan resisted scrubbing a hand down his face. He had enough of Alex mouthing off. He didn't need another alpha telling him how to run his clan. "Respectfully, Trent, truly respectfully, you can mind your own fucking business. What happens on this side of the fence, who I allow on my land, is my concern. Not yours."

A shadow passed over Trent's face. The lightness of his eyes faded back to his human color. Even the smell of fur lessened around him, replaced by a solid wall of caution. "Your business," he conceded. "Your funeral. Can't trust a human."

"I'll be sure to let you add that to my gravestone," Ethan growled. Aspersions cast upon Tansey made his bear want to fight. That need for action fed into his own. He wanted to work out his frustrations. Clan, cattle, lions, a woman… He expected the skies to open and a flash flood to rip through his land just to add another layer of awful to his life.

Trent scratched at his jaw. "Been wanting to catch up with you," he said begrudgingly. "Are you running trail rides for the tourists this year?"

"Depends. You offering up your horses?"

Ethan didn't want to do business with the man. He'd tried to set aside money and make plans to buy new mounts himself and do away with the need to work together. Trent was an even bigger asshole than Alex.

But four dead cows, and maybe four more, cut a bigger hole in his wallet. The trail ride money would be needed when Colette's tuition bill arrived or a horse threw a shoe or wolves broke his fences for the fifteenth time in a month. He couldn't count on his herd staying alive with the fucking Valdana pack picking them off.

Fuck it. Maybe he wouldn't need to worry about it much longer if Viho made his play and put him down.

Patches stepped to the side and tossed his head in agitation. Ethan stuffed his bear down before more than a growl and an intense need to bleed something surfaced.

Trent watched him with guarded eyes. "We can do five this time. One mare is due to foal soon."

"Five is just fine. You bringing them over, or should I send one of my boys?"

"You come this way. Give me a shout to firm up a time and day." Trent kneed his mount closer to the fence and stuck his hand across.

Ethan did the same and grasped the lion shifter's hand. "Pleasure doing business."

Trent scowled. "Doubt it. Don't turn my horses into nags, and send me your accounting each week. I won't have you skimming, Ashford."

Ethan bared his teeth in a rough approximation of a grin. He could curse Becca for setting him and Trent down the path of business partners.

One more problem to add to the heap.

As soon as Trent released his grip, he wheeled around and whistled for his men to follow. Ethan similarly rounded on Jesse and Alex.

"You two, get moving. I want the others found."

"What? You're still going?" Alex objected.

The growl he'd held in with Trent turned into a snarl directed at Alex. "I gave my word."

Alex glared back at him until Jesse crowded his horse between them. "Ride," Jesse snapped. "Now."

The brightness of Alex's eyes didn't fade as he spun his horse and trotted off. He wasn't a match for two bigger and more dominant bears, and he knew it.

"I'll try talking some sense into him," Jesse promised without prompting. "You go take care of your mate."

"She's not my mate," Ethan snapped as fiercely as Jesse before him.

"Alex is a lot of things, but he's not wrong in this. She caught your eye. Why else is she still alive after shooting at you?" His second dipped the brim of his hat in farewell. "Alpha."

Feeling spread too thin and called out on multiple fronts, Ethan kicked Patches toward home.

He gave his word to Tansey. That was all. He wouldn't bring a mate into the chaos of his life.

CHAPTER 9

Tansey sat on her hands to keep from fidgeting. The air in Ethan's truck was pleasant and oppressive all at once. He smelled delicious after a quick shower, but the air was like a thick blanket pressing down on her.

His eyes glowed, which she was certain meant he felt the same uneasy agitation she did. He tried to hide the silver under the brim of his cowboy hat—a new one, she noted, and not full of bullet holes. She almost felt guilty about that and stopped herself from offering to buy him a replacement twice.

Ethan slashed his eyes her way and tightened his hand around the steering wheel. Any tighter, and she imagined he'd crush the thing into smithereens.

"Thank you for this," she said to break the silence.

Ethan grunted.

Maybe it wasn't the air that was so heavy. Maybe it was the cowboy at her side ratcheting up her tension.

Whatever. She wasn't there to babysit his feelings. She was simply trying to find her brother. Ethan's problems were his own.

Still, she didn't like the silence. She didn't want to be an annoyance. She was a fixer by nature, and feeling the agitation in the air had her mentally reaching for a thousand possible solutions.

It was a relief when Ethan pulled into the parking lot of a small, brick building. Two police cruisers parked out front. Black block letters above the door named the place Bearden Police Department.

She doubted the building would suffice for a single precinct in Minneapolis.

Ethan hopped out of the truck and frowned when she shoved open her door before he could get around the hood. He beat her to the door of the station, though, and held that open for her with a ghost of a smile. "After you."

She opened her mouth to tell him that she was perfectly capable of opening her own doors, thank you very much, and stopped. He'd taken time out of his day to see her into town and make sure someone would talk to her. "Thank you," she said graciously and brushed past him.

She was almost certain he leaned forward and sniffed her hair.

The lobby wasn't much bigger than a handful of plastic chairs in front of a receptionist. A half-wall separated visitors from the desks of officers, with the entrance being a swinging door guarded by a bored gatekeeper.

Ethan leaned against the counter and drummed his fingers. "Jenny, is Judah around? We're here for our meeting."

"Sure is. Let me buzz him for you," she said.

Before she pressed a single button, a man appeared in the doorway of an office. "Ethan," he called, then strode forward. He smiled broadly and offered his hand. "Nice to see you without one of yours sitting in the drunk tank."

"We're working on it, Chief. Told Hunter he's on his own next time he's brawling over Joyce, so I think that'll buy us a week or two."

"That woman is pure trouble." Judah shook his head. "Who do you have for me here?"

Tansey straightened under the scrutiny and

offered her hand. She felt so small in comparison to the tall duo. The police chief had a firm grip, but not overly so. He minded his extra strength. "Tansey Nichols. My brother Rylan is missing."

"He's a shifter. Wolf, two months out," Ethan added.

Judah nodded sagely, then motioned them further into the station. They filed into an office, where Judah waved them into seats as he took his behind the desk. He wasted no time getting to the point. "What brings you to Bearden, Miss Nichols?"

Tansey took a deep breath and launched into her tale again. She started with knowing Rye's patterns, and getting worried when he abruptly stopped answering her calls and texts. She laid out her problems with the local police refusing to get involved with shifter problems, and how she came to employ Viho when all other options dwindled to nothing. She took Judah through the slow crawl out of Minnesota and all the way to Montana, one tiny clue or bit of scent at a time.

At the end of it, after taking the picture she passed across the desk, Judah leaned back in his chair and steepled his fingers. He looked from her to Ethan, who nodded once.

"Doubt Viho would willingly get near a police

station. The whole pack is banned from the enclave for picking pockets and fights, and that's just what we can pin on him." Judah punched a button on his desk phone. "Jenny, can you check the logs and see if Viho Valdana or any of his pack have contacted us? Or if anyone has reported a lone wolf on their territory?"

"Will do," Jenny answered through the intercom.

Relief tingled her scalp and worked through her tense muscles. Finally, someone was willing to do something. Actionable moves were being made. Maybe, just maybe, she'd find Rye and put an end to the most miserable chapter of her life.

Judah consulted the notes he'd jotted down while she spoke. "You arrived four days ago, correct? But your brother has been missing for a month?"

"I filed the missing person's paperwork like the local cops told me, but as soon as I mentioned he was a shifter they blew me off."

"Not the first time we've heard of that happening. I'm sorry you felt you were out of options." Judah made a face. "Did Rye give you any indication he had someone, or someones, he was planning to meet?"

Tansey stared at him for a long moment. The question was more polite than Hunter's the day before, but the meaning was just the same. "Why does everyone insist he's acting like some horny teenager?"

"Because, ma'am, he's a newly bitten shifter with instincts outside of his control. In essence, he *is* a horny teenager, and possibly one with an anger problem. If you do find him, you need to be careful. He needs our people right now to help him manage."

"I know Rye. He wouldn't hurt me."

"Tansey…" Ethan reached forward and squeezed her knee. "The man you know has a whole other entity inside him now. It can take months or years for a bitten shifter to gain full control. Rye might not hurt you, but his wolf is entirely capable of it."

Tansey sank into the comfort he offered her. His eyes didn't hold pity, just understanding. He didn't give her false condolences. Ethan gave her the facts without any sugar coating or unnecessary harshness. She appreciated his honesty.

"No offense intended," Judah said. "I'll make calls to the other enclaves and send them this picture. We'll do our best to find him. For you, it might be better to just head home and let the professionals do our jobs."

She jerked straight in her seat and brushed away Ethan's hand. "Fuck, no. I'm not leaving until I know Rye isn't here."

Judah and Ethan both sighed.

"No," she repeated fiercely. "I'll admit you're right that his wolf side could be a problem. But we've been each other's support for our entire lives. If there's even the slightest possibility that I can help him, I'm sticking around. I'll discuss the next steps when I know for sure he isn't in your town."

"Your choice, Miss Nichols. Leave your contact information with Jenny at the desk." Judah dismissed her and switched his focus. "Ethan?"

"I know. I'll keep an eye on her."

Tansey shot him a glare. She wasn't some little doll that needed tending.

"I think this one's capable of watching herself. No, I was going to say don't go starting trouble with the Valdanas."

An innocent look blossomed on Ethan's face. "Chief, you know I'd never do that. Finishing it is a whole other matter."

"Don't I know it." His eyes took on a hooded look. "Take care of yourselves. I'll be in touch."

The station door hadn't even fully closed behind her before her frustration burst out of her. "Well, that was as unproductive as anything else. At least Viho gave me an idea of where to look."

Ethan snorted. "Which was the wrong location, and then he shot at you."

"Or at you," she insisted.

"So he gave you wrong information and also failed at murder. Is that who you want working for you? Not the most reliable guy." He leaned against the front of his truck and watched her pace in front of him.

Despite herself, she chuckled. She dropped her head back with a heavy sigh and another bark of laughter. "No, I guess you're right. Not the most reliable of employees. Who can't get murder right?"

"Exactly. You'd think the alpha of a wolf pack motorcycle gang could at least do that correctly," Ethan deadpanned. His eyes softened and he reached forward to squeeze her shoulder. "Let Judah talk to his people and see what he can find. He's a good man. He won't take advantage of you."

Tansey pressed her lips together as a shiver worked its way down her spine. Ethan stroked his fingers in a gentle circle. Warmth spread through her, eating away at all the worry and frustration she'd carried for a month.

She wanted to believe him. She wanted to forget the sinking feeling in the pit of her stomach. How he swept away her concerns and replaced them with a bit of hope, she didn't know. Magic, maybe. She could use a little pixie dust and an afternoon of zero trouble.

She peeked up to find impossibly bright blue eyes watching her. The color slowly faded into gorgeous silver with a hint of hungry promise. Tansey's heart thudded against her ribcage as her gaze remained locked with the handsome cowboy's.

Maybe there was one man she did want taking advantage.

The roar of a motorcycle engine reached her ears just before Viho swung into the parking lot with his hair streaming behind him.

Tansey jumped back like she'd been caught with her hand in the cookie jar. Guilt swelled to life. She blinked once, twice, her head clearing of whatever bad ideas Ethan planted there.

Her brother was missing. She didn't have time for anything else.

Viho killed the rumbling bike and kicked down the stand. "Girl, if you wanted to slum it, you didn't need to sink this low."

Ethan growled and stepped in front of her. "Turn around and get out of town, wolf," he ordered.

"Or what, bear? You going to turn your territory

red with blood?" Viho grinned. "Red enough as it is with all your cows dying, ain't it?"

The growls from both men cranked up by the second. Tansey thought she could feel the noise vibrating in her chest. Even the air grew heavier the longer they stared one another down.

Ethan told her Viho wanted his land, but the hatred bubbling between them spoke of many more issues than that. The two had obvious beef with one another and were just looking for an excuse to let fists and fangs fly.

Every instinct screamed *danger* in big, bright, neon letters. She didn't want to be anywhere near them when they finally boiled over.

She reached forward and grabbed Ethan's forearm. His eyes didn't leave Viho, nor did his growl cease. He shook her off, so she tugged on him. "Ethan," she whispered harshly. "Let's just go."

"Go?" Viho snapped. "You're not going anywhere until I get my cut."

"Your cut for what?" Tansey hissed and rounded on him. "Ethan didn't know where my brother was. He's given me more help in a day than your entire month."

"This your new scam, Viho? Make someone

disappear and then charge the family a finder's fee for the location of the body?" Ethan added.

"You'd know about making someone disappear, wouldn't you?" Viho snarled. "You Ashfords are all the same breed of traitor."

Ethan's fists balled up tight. His lips raised with a snarl. "Same can be said of the Valdana infestation."

Whoo, boy. Those words were laced with an unfathomable amount of hatred. Viho's answering growl rippled fear down her spine and she was reminded—again—that she was a human and both men had beasts under their skin.

Tansey tugged on Ethan's arm again. One more try, then she was retreating into the police station and letting them brawl it out. She wasn't afraid of a fight, but she was fond of her limbs remaining attached to her body.

Viho glanced over their shoulders and toward the door of the station. He fired up his bike again, then pointed at her. "Your new man can't be trusted. Remember that. It's in his fucking blood."

CHAPTER 10

E than laced his fingers behind his neck and glared after the asshole on the bike. He hadn't allowed his bear to taste the fucker's blood, so he hoped Viho would wipe out and feel the horrors of road rash before slamming face first into a tree.

At least he had confirmation the pack was behind picking off his herd. He had the scents, and now he had the words. They'd pay for his loss, one way or another.

Viho's final jab enraged him even more than the unnecessary death of his cattle. In his blood? Fuck that. A fresh growl rolled through him, along with the need to fight. His skin prickled with the brush of fur.

He wasn't his old man, and he certainly wasn't

living his life stuck in the past or according to old rules. His father's mistakes and habits were dead and buried.

Ethan worked his ass off to keep his word to his people. Viho wasn't one of them and he needed to clear out and wreck someone else's life. Traitor? Never. Defender of his fucking clan and land to the death.

Tansey pressed a palm to his chest. Concern covered over the honey of her scent. "Are you okay?"

Damn her, he wasn't the one needing that question. She had a missing brother to worry about. His troubles weren't hers.

"Fine," he said between gritted teeth. His bear still slashed at him, but her hand on his chest took the edge off the beast's rage.

The touch came with an unwanted side effect. He itched to wrapped his hand around her wrist and hold her there forever.

Or in her hair as he guided her lower.

"You're still growling."

Ethan's bear cut the noise so sharply that he felt like a rubber band snapped inside him. The animal even had the gall to chuff at him for making their mate worried.

Worse still, all Ethan wanted to do was soothe

the worry from Tansey's expression. He wanted to provide for her, ease her mind, make sure she never had an unpleasant day ever again. Her big, whiskey-brown eyes shining up at him only made him want it more.

He scrubbed a hand down his face and blew out a heavy breath. Quirking an eyebrow at her, he said, "I need a drink. How about you?"

"Don't you need to get back to the ranch? You made it sound super important this morning."

"The others can handle repairing a fence and tracking down some missing cows." And he didn't want to let her out of his sight when the wolf knew who had her.

How had she done that? She'd triggered his need to protect what he deemed his. Hell, underneath the disappointment of her sticking around, his bear had cheered.

Her hand still burned against his chest. He wrapped his fingers around her wrist, as delicate as a bird compared to his. "One drink. We'll toast the start of a real search."

Tansey dropped her hand and searched the sky for an answer. "One drink," she conceded. "That's all I'll let you talk me into. I've taken up enough of your time today as it is."

"This coming from the woman who practically bit my head off when I left this morning."

"I have the right to change my mind after watching the clock tick by slowly. You didn't need to hold my hand and wait with me."

No. She wasn't one to let others wait on her. She did the caring on her terms, like hauling around with Viho in search of her closest relation.

The silence on the short drive to The Roost took on a different note than leaving the ranch. Then, she'd been all agitation and tension. The tension still hung heavy around her, but there were notes of hope in her scent. She didn't fidget as much, either, which made the air easier to breathe. His fault, that. His bear didn't like seeing her in such a state. The creature wanted to bite everything that moved.

Just like before, Tansey jumped out of the truck before he could round the hood and escort her down properly. She didn't beat him to the door, though, which let him inhale her honeyed scent. He stuffed that victory in his pocket. His mother taught him to be a gentleman, even if he had a monster growling in his middle.

The place was almost a home away from home. There was a shittier bar closer to Black Claw that would do in a pinch if he needed to wet his throat or throw something back to take the edge off from some dumb stunt one of his clan pulled. The Roost was where the tourists and most of the locals went to get their fun and drinks.

Tansey's eyes adjusted while he zeroed in on the woman behind the bar. Leah leaned against the counter, one hand casually rubbing her huge stomach and eyes carefully watching one of the regulars start his afternoon of drinking.

"Aren't you supposed to pop soon?" He impressed himself with keeping the strangled notes out of his voice.

His bear ran full steam ahead with his sendings. Image after image was shoved into Ethan's head because of the stupid creature under his skin. Every last one of them were of Tansey with a belly as big as Leah's and a smile just for him.

Fucking instincts.

Leah eyed him sharply. "I'm not a balloon, and now your drinks cost double."

"Worth every penny to be served by the best bartender in town." He flashed her his second best smile.

"You're back to regular price, but you're tipping for two so make it good." Leah rubbed a hand over her stomach, then turned her attention to Tansey. "And who's your date?"

"It's not a date," they both said, entirely too quickly.

"Tansey," he introduced right on the heels of his fuck up. "This is Leah. The usual for me, and whatever the lady is having."

"Your best stout," Tansey answered. She turned to him, her eyes dancing. "What? Expected some fancy girly drink?"

"I honestly don't know what to expect with you."

Her head cocked to the side and her lips pursed together like she didn't know what to make of his comment. That made two of them.

Leah's lips hitched into a grin as she pushed pints across the bar. "Yeah, okay, not-daters. What brings you to town, Tansey?"

"Missing brother. Ethan offered to help."

"Did he?" Leah arched an eyebrow. "Well, good luck. I hope he's not missing for long."

A pang of sadness wafted off Tansey. Ethan ripped the little cocktail napkin under his pint to shreds.

Tansey ran a finger around the edge of her glass as the foam head dissolved down. She cast a quick glance his way under her thick eyelashes. "Have you always lived in Bearden?"

Tension tightened his chest, different than being locked in a truck with her scent in his nose. They were treading into new territory. His bear wanted to dive right in and figure out every piece of the puzzle that was Tansey Nichols. He wanted to hold back.

Not answering her was impolite. The question wasn't more than surface. Ask anyone he grew up with, and they could give her the answer. "Born and raised out on the ranch. Cow and horses have been in my family since my great-grandfather put up fences and called some land his. Black Claw was my father's, and now it's mine."

"It's a huge house for that many people."

"Wasn't always just us. My father's clan was bigger, and my mother rented out rooms for a little while. What about you? What did you do in the big city?"

"Whatever I needed to get by. My family struggled, and I vowed as soon as I turned eighteen I'd make the load lighter for my mom. So I hightailed it out of our tiny little town and got a job waitressing. Then there was housekeeping at a motel. More diner work, where I had the pleasure of managing the kitchen. Last gig was catering events for a hoity-toity country club."

Once again, he found himself impressed with her. She wasn't afraid of hard work to help out someone else. The quality was one he needed in a mate.

She continued, "One of my contacts recently purchased this adorable little inn upstate and has been trying to lure me to be her head chef. It got me thinking about my own future, you know. Not getting any younger."

"You're right. You'll be an old hag before you know it. Better start collecting cats."

"Ethan Ashford, did you just make a joke? I was so sure you were one of those strong, silent types that didn't know the first thing about humor." She watched him in the mirror behind the bar, smile twitching her lips even as her tone stayed flat.

"I can joke. I have a sense of humor."

Ethan wanted to strangle his damn bear. Or press his nose into the crook of Tansey's neck and drown in her scent.

The silence stretched between them. Damn it all. He wasn't as awkward as a teenager on his first date with any of the women he met at the height of the bar's nightlife. Words and charm flowed freely then.

All surface. Too much surface. He wanted to get beneath the waves.

He asked the first question that popped into his mind. "What would you die for?"

Motherfucker.

"What would I die for? That's kind of a morbid question, isn't it?" She drew shapes into the condensation of her glass. "Death isn't exactly what I'm thinking about. If I had to pick, I guess I'd say my brother? My mother? Here, how about this?" She sat up straighter and adopted the breathy voice of a beauty contestant. "World peace."

Ethan barked a laugh, and she relaxed. "Look, no one is going to need my death for their survival. So how about you, Mr. Unfair Questions? What would you die for?"

"Putting me on the spot. Okay, that's fair." He nodded twice, then gave his answer. "Colette, hands down. She's got a future in front of her and I'm doing everything in my power to make sure she never has the worries I did when I was her age."

"Sounds like you two are as close as me and Rye."

"Mmm," he said around his glass. "Happens when you're forced to be the parent."

A frown pulled down her lips. "That's the worst, isn't it? My dad abandoned the family. Yours?"

"Fell into the bottle after my mom passed." He shrugged. It was rough, and he still hated the old man daily, but it molded him.

He never liked talking about those years. More than the vaguest of details sent his bear snarling away inside him. Not with Tansey. She made him want to open up about the struggles and the wins.

She swiveled in her seat. Concern wavered in her scent again. For him.

Ethan turned to her, bracketing her knees with his. The slight brush of their legs together rolled energy over his skin. His hands shot forward and grabbed hers. A current whipped through him at the touch, obliterating every cell of objection and reconstructing him with pure need for the mysterious woman.

He dropped her hands and looked her pity square in the face with a challenge to call him out. No amount of whining changed the past. He worked hard to better the future.

And no amount of brushing against silky soft skin changed the fact that he didn't want a mate.

But she didn't say a word. Tansey cocked her head again like she saw something interesting.

His bear echoed the motion.

Curious, that. After the words with Viho, he

expected the beast to keep on raging until he could shift and direct that anger elsewhere. The clan were always down for a brawl. The pent-up energy and lifelong fury could be unleashed on them.

Instead, the bear just watched and listened and tested the air. The brief flurry of sendings ceased as Tansey talked. Ethan couldn't remember a time where his inner animal wasn't pushing for something.

Tansey licked her lips and inhaled steadily, swiveling back to the bar. "So why don't you rent out rooms anymore? Is it because you all suck at cooking?"

"Woman," he snorted, "is that any way to offer thanks for the meal you were provided?"

"I'm not sure if a terrible chili counts as a meal. Do you just dump cans bought back in the seventies and call it dinner?"

"You think you can do better?"

"Oh, I know I can. You'll be singing my praises at first bite." She grinned and took a pull from her glass. "But really, why?"

"My bears are not fit for civilization. Jesse and Lorne could probably stay steady. Alex would shred the guests' belongings in five minutes."

"Too bad about your man-eating bears. You basically have the perfect setup. Extra rooms, from what I saw. Land galore to turn the tourists out to play. Hipsters aren't solely focused on their organically grown coffee beans and craft beers. They want authentic life experiences. You can give them a dude ranch and rake in the cash."

The thought was nice, but impossible. His mother was around to take care of any house concerns while his father worked with others outside. There weren't enough hours in the day to add babying guests to the daily schedule. "Except we'd be poisoning anyone that tried to stomach our revolting menu."

Tansey's eyes laughed at him. "Let me cook for you guys tonight. It's the least I can do."

"After shooting at me, accusing me of kidnapping, and being an all-around disturber of the peace?" Her smile widened like he'd thrown her compliments. Maybe they were, for a woman like her. Tough on the outside, with a caring streak a mile wide. "Tell me, is that offer purely as an apology, or is it because you're saving your taste buds?"

"Why not both?" She shrugged. She swallowed down the last of her beer and shook a finger at him. Sassy girl. "And that's your one drink."

Ethan chuckled. She bounced from one thought

to the next without any hint of where she'd take him next. Confusing, intriguing woman. Guarded, too. He could press her if she switched directions, but he liked the wild chase.

He shoved away from the bar and threw down a couple bills. "One drink. Now you'll relieve me of my servitude?"

"Back to the dirt and manure with you, cowboy."

Her foot caught on the stool as she hopped off. Ethan clamped his hands on her shoulders and steadied her before she fell. He should pull away. He needed to let go. The heat that unfurled under his palms was like metal forging them together.

A beat. Her throat worked with a swallow. "Was this your plan all along, Ashford? Get me liquored up?"

Ethan did his best to hide his smile, then gave up. She got his best one. "Depends, Nichols. Is it working or do I need to order a round of shots to go with your one beer?"

Tansey didn't pull away or twist out of his grasp. She stared up at him with her gorgeous big eyes and time seemed to slow. The connection forged between them began to spiral and drew him closer.

Ethan leaned down and hovered over her lips for a breath.

The first brush of her lips sent a jolt of electricity surging down his spine. Fire rolled through him. He growled. She gasped.

He was lost.

Ethan locked a hand behind her neck and dragged her closer. Good skies above, she tasted so good, felt so soft. She moved with him slowly, twisting her tongue against his as he deepened the kiss.

A sexy little noise worked its way out of her chest and his cock jumped in response.

Mine.

Fuck.

Tansey wrapped her arms around Ethan's neck. Holy hot damn, the man could kiss. Tingles of electricity ran up and down her arms and all the way to her toes. Toes that curled, by the way. Her mother always said to beware a man that could curl her toes, because he would steal her heart and all her sense.

Yep, that advice was out the window. She didn't want to stop even to come up for air.

Ethan held her so close she could feel all the hard muscles she'd seen since she tried to shoot some information out of him. Even more, she felt every hard inch of him that her body practically begged for. Her knees would have knocked together and she'd have fallen if it weren't for his grip on her neck and waist. His fingers massaged her wherever they touched and further coaxed her into... whatever they were doing.

The longer she spent with him, the more smiles he flashed her way, the worse she had it for him. He was nice, if rough around the edges. That had its own appeal, though. Not in a need-to-fix sort of way. He could hold his own through the worst of times and still give her a kiss on the cheek at the end of the day.

He helped her, too. When no one else could give her solid answers, when her last hope bled her savings and screwed her over, Ethan was the one to set the wheels in motion to find her brother. He set aside his own responsibilities and ushered her into his life.

She could let herself like him. Just a smidge. That was as far as it could go. Toe-curling kisses and warmth pooling in her belly were the perfect compromise.

Her body felt flushed and feverish when Ethan finally let her go with a lingering sip of her lips.

She didn't think she'd ever been so thoroughly claimed.

Ethan swam into her unfocused view, cocky smirk gracing his lips. She let him have it. He earned it.

The tripping beat of her heart didn't slow as he reached forward and brushed a bit of hair over her ear. "Damn, Nichols. Couldn't wait for a little privacy?" he teased with a flash of his perfect smile.

Another flush whipped through her and Tansey quickly glanced around the mostly empty bar. Leah hovered at the other end with the only other patron and looked elsewhere so quickly Tansey knew they'd been noticed.

Her eyes bounced everywhere but the cowboy in front of her, then settled in one spot. The flames he'd ignited inside her froze to solid ice. Chills ran up and down her spine and lifted the fine hairs all along her body.

"What the fuck is that?"

Clearly, it wasn't the reaction he intended. Confusion wrinkled his forehead, then shock smoothed everything out. Blank offense tightened his jaw and narrowed his eyes.

Tansey pointed over his shoulder at the picture tacked on the wall with a mess of others. They were all poses and faces she'd seen while out with friends, and probably even made herself. Nights of fun and debauchery were forever enshrined for other patrons to see.

But one held her entire attention. She jabbed her finger at it again.

"Rye was here. With you."

Ethan twisted to look over his shoulder.

In the photo, Rye and Ethan had their arm's thrown over each other's shoulders. Both wore well lubricated grins and unfocused eyes.

Viho warned her. He wasn't innocent in anything, that was obvious. But he warned her about Ethan and her stupid, traitorous ovaries muddied her brain and made her overlook the red flags everyone kept closely guarded, Ethan more than most.

She'd just locked lips with someone who denied ever knowing Rye.

The betrayal stung, despite all her reasonings. She didn't know Ethan, could only take him at his word. He'd convinced her he could help and was involved all along.

Was he laughing at her the entire time? Stringing her along when he knew the fate of her brother? Taking her to the fucking scene of the crime?

Good lord, she'd been an idiot to try bonding with him. The brief moment where she let herself feel a tiny bit of hope that Rye would be found and she would get her answers were for nothing. Ethan was a liar and a fraud, just like every other man she'd let get close. Worse, because he hid the most important person in her life from her.

She'd kissed him. Her stomach turned.

Ethan whirled back around. "I know how this looks—"

Tansey melted all her hurt into fiery anger. "No shit. It looks like you had a wild time with my brother, who then disappeared off the face of the planet. What did you do, bury him out on your ranch and pray no one turned up looking for him?"

"Tansey, listen to me." He grabbed her arms and ducked down to snag her eyes with his. "I don't even remember that night. I couldn't tell you if it was a month or a year ago."

"Most of these are shots of tourists," Leah added, summoned by the outburst. "They like getting loaded and taking photos with shifters. It could have been something like that. We get a lot of traffic these days."

Tansey snapped her head toward the other

woman. "You're just defending your own kind," she spat.

Her skin crawled with Ethan's continued grip. She forced herself a step back, then another.

She needed air. She needed to find Rye. She needed to get away from Ethan Ashford.

Tansey spun on her heel and nearly ran for the door.

"Tansey. Tansey, stop." Ethan stepped in front of her, distress lining every inch of him.

"Fuck off. I don't have time for liars." She tried to step past him, but he darted in front of her again.

"It's not safe," he said with conviction. "Viho could try to get to you. Come back to the ranch."

"I'm not stepping foot on your ranch again. I'll find my own place in town." He didn't move, so she planted her hands on his chest and shoved. He didn't budge, but at least he let her walk past him. "Leave me the fuck alone, Ethan."

She didn't dare turn back around or probe why her heart hurt so bad.

CHAPTER 11

E than laced his fingers behind his neck and watched Judah's officers crawl over his ranch. One held his clan apart, then led each out of earshot to ask questions. His barn had already been combed through from top to bottom, and no one appreciated him suggesting they could muck the stalls while they were in there.

At least no big, black SUV had accompanied them. Even with the Supernatural Enforcement Agency supposedly swinging in a new direction, he wanted nothing to do with them. Cops he knew and mostly respected were enough of a problem without the damn feds breathing down his neck.

An irritated growl tickled the back of his throat

as he rounded on Chief Hawkins. "It was her, wasn't it?"

"You know I can't give you that information." Judah plastered patience on his face.

"Who else would it be, Chief?" The fury in Tansey's eyes and scent still stung. She was determined to find her brother, so it was only a matter of time before the police knocked down his door. He didn't expect it so soon after their failed date.

"We received a report that the missing person had a connection to you. We're following up."

"She shoved that picture under your nose and told you to move." He scrubbed a hand down his face, then flung his arm out to gesture at the scene with frustration. "How many times have you and your clan been called to the bar because someone got too drunk? How many tourists are in and out of there every night? By the Broken, how many other pictures are pinned to that wall where I'm in the background? I don't remember the guy."

"As I said, we're following up on all tips. I appreciate your cooperation in the matter."

A broken fucking record, that's all Judah was. His calm tone made Ethan's bear want to act up and get any other reaction.

The bear had been wild ever since Tansey threw

her sucker punch of accusations his way. He thought they were getting somewhere. She'd let her guard down enough for him to see the shining center beyond her tough-girl walls. And that kiss! Hot damn, he craved another fix. Just thinking about it had his cock straining against his zipper.

Chances of that happening were as likely as the brother being found on his ranch.

"Where is she staying?"

The deputies talking to his clan finished up and stomped a path toward his home. Ethan's jaw ticked to let them paw through his den, but the invasive search didn't end at his porch.

From threat to kiss to pain in his ass, Tansey had wrecked his routine in less than a day. He'd been right to avoid anything more serious than a night.

Judah snorted. "I'm not telling you that, either."

"If it's not Muriel's, then it has to be the cabins at the crest. Unless she found a spot with all the humans, or someone opened a room for her. Just make this easy on me."

"That's nothing you need to know."

"Can you at least tell me if she went back to Viho?"

His bear snarled at the idea.

Ethan wanted to wash his hands of the troublesome woman. She'd been nothing put problems in a pretty package since she drove onto his land and took a shot at him. Damn him, but he didn't wish her any danger. Viho was sure to hurt her if she got near him again.

Fucking Viho. He'd planted the whole, insane idea in Tansey's head. And for what? Nothing could be proved against him. No body would be found because he didn't know the missing brother.

Viho was out for blood. He wanted to toy with him. Drive him crazier by the second. Needling him into reacting when he should be protecting. Fucker. He'd rather see the ranch burn to the ground than give one inch of it to an asshole wolf with zero claim.

He had no doubt that Viho's parting words were heavy in Tansey's mind, too.

Judah watched him with a hooded expression and arms crossed over his chest. Even his scent was unreadable and shifty. Hopeful. Wary. Surprised.

"Viho has not been spotted inside the enclave, and you heard Miss Nichols' intentions this morning."

So she was still around. One hell of a roundabout way to say she wasn't in danger of Viho ripping her throat out for talking to the cops.

At least his bear stopped tearing him to shreds and a bit of the tightness in his chest faded. The beast was only mildly pissed. Ethan took it as a win. His week wasn't complete without the animal throwing a tantrum over the wind changing direction.

"Listen, stay out of town for a few days. Cool off. I have enough trouble with tourists trying to tap a vein, and now this Valdana mess." Judah shot a look toward his officers, then turned his back and drew Ethan a little further away. "Keep Hunter locked down, too. Found out this afternoon one of my deputies has been seeing Joyce on the side."

"I'll let him down easy," Ethan answered wryly. Damn the woman, and damn Hunter for letting her walk all over him.

"Good. Now, let me get through this without any problems. We can check this box and be done."

"What about her stuff? You won't tell me where she's at, so is someone going to get her car and clothes off my property?"

"Arrangements will be made." Judah sighed. "Consider what I said. Stick close to home for a few days and let this blow over."

Ethan sprawled onto one of the benches lining the porch and stretched his long legs in front of him. As a final rejection of any threat Judah's cops and clan posed to him, he slid his Stetson down over his eyes and folded his hands over his chest.

There was nothing to consider. He was done with Tansey Nichols. Her possessions would be gone as soon as his home and land were found free of any missing brother. He could get back to his version of normal with bears that needed to brawl every damn day. His only concern would be keeping Black Claw afloat.

Any wolf caught fucking with his herd would be ripped to pieces and left for the scavengers.

Boots thunked up the steps. The earthy aroma all bears carried twisted around identifiable thick spices. Ethan didn't bother lifting his hat.

"This on your girl?" Jesse asked.

"She ain't my girl," Ethan snapped. All the serene calm he wore as a fuck-you to the Hawkins clan disappeared as he stiffened and jerked his hat into place.

Jesse shrugged. "You left together, and came back alone. Lawman shows up as we're winding down for the day. Can't help but see a connection."

"She found a picture at The Roost of me and her brother together."

"So that's why they were asking how often you leave the ranch without one of us tagging along."

"This is for the best. With Viho culling our herd and trail rides starting up, there's no time for distractions. Judah involved and her out of our hair is the best conclusion."

Images whirled into his mind from his bear. The beast snarled with each one, but didn't stem the flow. Tansey belonged to them. Separated left her alone and in danger. The woman wandering the woods with wolves lurking in the darkness was plain enough to decipher.

Ethan kicked the rebellious creature to the back of his head.

"She's not a distraction if she's your mate. Everything else is secondary to her."

"You go take a swing at her if you're so interested." A growl rattled in his chest and his lips lifted in a silent snarl.

Jesse quieted and tilted his head to the side in a show of submission.

"If she's my mate, she'll understand the pressure we're under year after year. That's how it's supposed to be, right? Perfection between two people?"

"Now you sound like a child," his second chided. Another tilt of his head exposed his neck. He knew he pushed even his limits granted by the position and years of familiarity. "You know that's not how it works. Even mates have their fights and hurdles to jump. The willingness to keep doing that and stay in love sets them apart."

"Love is just a drug and addictions are a road to ruin. I'm not looking to fall apart as soon as I don't get my fix." His chest ached. He resisted the urge to rub at the pain and tension. No relief would come.

The pain was all bullshit anyway. Instincts gone haywire. He'd be fine just as soon as he lost the memory of her honeyed scent and the taste on his lips. A bottle of whiskey and a welcoming stranger at the bar would do the trick.

His entire body tensed in revulsion.

Ethan slouched back into his posture of uncaring and slid his hat over his eyes. "We still have a ranch to run and cattle to protect. I'll take first watch tonight," he said gruffly.

Jesse waited a few seconds more, then stomped off the porch.

He couldn't do anything about Tansey or her stubborn conviction that he had information on her brother's whereabouts, but he could watch for Viho. Dammit, he'd take that threat from her life if he lined up the shot.

CHAPTER 12

Tansey pursed her lips and watched Chief Hawkins ease into the police station parking lot from her spot just down the street. He came from a different direction than the past four mornings and pulled his cruiser around the building. He didn't poke back around the corner to enter through the front, so he must have taken a back door.

She twisted the key in her ignition and zipped down the street and into the same spot she'd parked in every damn morning since Ethan brought her there.

The man's face flashed heat through her mind. He'd become a black hole since she pushed her way out of the bar and left him gaping at her like a fish. He hadn't tried to find her and she couldn't get any updates about him from the Chief of Police. She normally wouldn't care, except he was the prime suspect in Rye's disappearance.

Tansey blasted through the gate separating the tiny lobby and the rest of the police station. The handful of officers lifted their heads, but didn't bother getting up. Jenny just rolled her eyes and went back to filing her nails.

She locked on to her target coming out of the break room. "You're avoiding me!"

Judah lifted his hands, warding her off with a steaming mug of coffee and a file folder. "There is nothing new to tell you, Miss Nichols."

Tansey followed his retreat into his office. "Why isn't that man sitting in your cell?"

"As you've been told, we followed up on your information and found no signs of your brother." Judah set his mug down and then placed his folder in the exact middle of his desk. His hands folded over top as soon as he seated himself.

"He lied about knowing Rye! What else could he be lying about? Maybe he has some murder shack out on some desolate corner of his ranch and that's where Rye was taken."

"I assure you that's not the case."

"And Viho? Why haven't you talked to him yet?"

"We're still conducting interviews, Miss Nichols," he said flatly.

His weaselly answers just made her angrier. "So you can't find him. Top notch detective work, Hawkins. You'll find my brother in no time with that work ethic."

Judah slammed to his feet, bumping his desk in his haste and spilling his coffee. His hand wrapped around her upper arm before she could react. He hauled her to her feet. His hard grip didn't give her any choice but to move or be dragged like a tantruming toddler.

Tansey stomped her way to the door and back out into the parking lot. She rubbed at her arm as soon as he released her. She wouldn't be surprised if she bruised.

"We will contact you when we have new information," Judah said between clenched teeth. "Have a pleasant day. Away from my station."

Tansey glared at Judah's retreating back and the glass shaking in the slammed door. She stalked around her car, kicked at a tire, and let off a scream of frustration.

Maybe she'd gone too far with sassing Judah. That didn't warrant being dragged out of the police station. She'd been looking for her brother for a solid month and nobody seemed willing to do anything! Not the local cops, not Viho, and now Judah found his place on the list.

Of them all, she hated to admit, Ethan was the only one to actually get her somewhere. He put her in front of Judah and outed Viho as a snake. Sure, he did it with his own—likely criminal—knowledge, but it was actionable information no one else provided.

The hot ball of frustration and her foot throbbed together. Tansey yanked open her car door and slid inside, not knowing where to go.

She circled slowly through one neighborhood, then another. She wanted to get a feel for the town and have an understanding of where someone might go to disappear. All she'd gotten were suspicious looks for her creeptastic investigation.

Most neighborhoods were exactly like the ones she grew up in. Some were richer than others, some had messier yards, but they were all homes.

Then there were the private drives that looked like cul-de-sacs from her vantage point on the street. Houses clustered together, usually around some center point. She thought those belonged to clans like Ethan's.

Regardless of their positioning, none contained her brother. She'd driven around and poked her nose where it didn't belong since an officer handed over her keys and said her bag was in the backseat. Nothing was missing inside. She checked. Ethan might be a disappearing murderer, but he wasn't a thief.

After more than an hour of aimless wandering that put her no closer to finding Rye, her stomach grumbled. She found a parking spot reserved for guests staying at Muriel's and hopped out, trying to figure out what she wanted to eat. She took off across the town square.

She'd been so focused on finding Rye and learning the nooks and crannies of a new town that she hadn't stopped to really *look* at the place.

Adorable. Cozy. She bet with snow on the ground and smoke curling out of fireplaces, it could be featured on the poster of any cheesy holiday movie that was secretly a sinister horror full of abductees being ground into sausage by the unassuming side character at the edge of town.

Tansey unclenched her fists and tried to shake off her frustrations.

Spring was just beginning to take hold in Bearden, and nothing made that more apparent than the gathering of people in the green town square and meandering up and down Main Street.

On one side of the road, a woman quickly wrote down an order and dashed through the doors of a busy coffee shop. Another kicked out a wooden sign and scrawled the daily special in chalk and decorated it with flowers and steaming mugs.

Opposite Mug Shot, a surly man frowned from the window of Tommy's Diner, then taped up a printed sheet of paper. Tansey squinted and chuckled. NO SPECIALS. JUST ORDER, the sign read.

Further down, the firefighters pulled a big red fire truck out of the building and crawled all over it. Then out came the buckets and soap suds, and Tansey understood the gathered onlookers choosing to take their coffee on the patio seats. The trash talk thrown from one man to another quickly turned their sponges into weapons and left more than one shirt clinging to heavily muscled bodies. One more walked out of the bay, shook his head, and walked right back inside.

Rye would have hated it and relentlessly mocked the idyllic scenery. The tourists snapping photos would be the subject of ridicule. Tansey could almost hear him label the place a stifling tourist trap. So how did he wind up in the small town?

The question was an extension of all the rest. The whys piled up in her head right along with the hows. Why did he leave? How could he not let her know?

Her hurtful inner voice chose that moment to claw to the front of her mind. The answer to her questions was the same. She drove him away.

Tansey sucked in a breath and pushed back on the stinging doubt. She couldn't let it eat at her. There was hope. She needed to learn patience. Rye would be found.

"That's her."

Tansey cast a glance over her shoulder. The trio of elderly women she'd passed leaned in and whispered to one another. A whisper to them, anyway. She heard them clear as day.

"Missing brother, I hear. She's been harassing Judah Hawkins all week, poor boy."

Tansey nearly snorted. Judah wasn't some wizened codger, but he was definitely not a boy.

"Did you hear the McNamaras out on Still Wind Road had their shed broken into? I wonder if the two are related."

Cheeks burning, Tansey whirled on the trio. "What was that?"

They didn't slow. The one in the middle fixed her with a warm smile as they passed. "Oh, good morning dear. I hope you're enjoying your stay with us."

Tansey narrowed her eyes at the fake niceties. "Just lovely," she said between gritted teeth. "Everyone is so polite and friendly."

Mostly true. At least they had the grace to gossip quietly if they did so at all.

The leader nodded with her viperous smile still on her face and let one of the others open the diner door for her.

Tansey spun on her heel and stalked back up the street. Being tossed from one establishment was enough for the day and she didn't want to hold her tongue.

Luckily, with lunch approaching, Hogshead Joint had its doors thrown open to lure in passersby with the mouthwatering scent of barbecue.

Wanting to avoid any more gossip, Tansey took a seat at the far end of the bar. She cracked open her wallet and scowled, then placed an order for the cheapest sandwich combo on the menu.

She'd need to pick up a shift somewhere if she intended to stay any longer, or she'd find herself cozy in the back seat of her car at night. Not the first time, and she was sure it wouldn't be the last.

She'd tried to keep moths from fluttering out of

her wallet by working whenever Viho stopped for more than a day or two. Keeping busy was better than staring at cheap motel artwork and imagining how her brother met his end. And that was better than socializing with the Vagabonds.

Maybe Muriel would be kind enough to give her a closet to sleep in as exchange for helping in the kitchen and changing out the guest linens. The work was the kind she wanted to do in her own bed-and-breakfast one day.

The one day dream shrank down to a distant pinpoint the longer she stayed on the move.

She just needed to make ends meet for a little while longer. As soon as she could be convinced Rye wasn't in Bearden, she'd make her way back to a lonely apartment and wait for someone to give her a call.

Tansey hated the idea of giving up on her brother. Something ugly crawled up her spine and settled deep in her brain. Staying in Bearden felt like the last hope of seeing Rye again, but other than a single picture and the word of an outlaw, there was no sign of him.

She'd been boxed in, and she needed time to rebuild her options. A steady paycheck would be useful. She could save up to hire someone else to take the case. A retired detective, maybe. Someone with more credentials than Viho and more credibility than Ethan.

Speak of the devil.

Ethan sauntered through the door like the embodiment of cocksure cowboy.

She hated and loved every step he took. She didn't want to be anywhere near the man and couldn't help but get an eyeful of him.

Dark jeans clung to his thick thighs, just like the days she'd been with him. She thought he had a collection of denim made specifically for him. She knew the deep green t-shirt that stretched over his chest hid a mass of muscle. The brim of his cowboy hat hid his eyes. Blue, or silver, she wondered.

Tansey hunched in on herself and cut her inspection short.

Not good enough. A quick peek found him abruptly stopped on his path toward the bar. He lifted his face slightly and his nostrils flared.

Shit.

Ethan fixed his eyes on her and stalked toward her with the lethal grace of a predator determined to catch his prey.

He leaned against the bar on his elbows and

swiveled his head in her direction. "What are you doing here?" he asked in a low voice.

"Just trying to have a peaceful meal. Which you're ruining."

Ethan mumbled something under his breath and adjusted his hat. "I meant in town. Shouldn't you have run back home by now?"

Tansey took an obnoxiously loud slurp from her straw and popped her lips when she finished. "What's the saying? Friends close, enemies closer?"

Ethan struck as fast as any snake, unwinding to his full height and wrapping his hand around her arm. Something silly like digging in her heels didn't stop him. He maneuvered her between the few occupied tables and out onto the empty deck.

Huh. She didn't know the place was so big or had such a lovely view of the river.

Too bad it was ruined by the big brute probably intending to toss her over the side.

"Would you stop? I've been shoved around enough for one day."

The hand on her arm didn't let go, but his grip loosened. His eyes darted to her skin. "Who did this?" he demanded in a growl, blue eyes going to icy silver in a flash.

"Don't worry about it," she hissed and jerked out of his grasp.

He replaced his hand immediately, stroking fingers over the marks. Warmth flared to life at the spot and spread through her like sinking into a hot bath.

"Tansey." Her name on his lips was pure gravel that sank right to her middle and demanded her undivided attention. "Who?"

A shiver worked through her body. "Chief Hawkins," she answered in a rush.

"Good girl." Another growl rumbled out of Ethan. "He shouldn't have done this. Especially not to you."

She didn't want his praise or his sympathy. Not even the tingles spreading across her skin would make her admit otherwise.

"I happen to bruise easy and none of you brutes know your own strength." She slapped away his hand and made a face. "I—*maybe*—deserved to get dragged out of the station."

Ethan stared down at her, then cracked a stunning smile. "Now, that I believe. What did you say?"

"I asked why you weren't in a jail cell." His face fell and she used the moment to put more distance

WRANGLED FATE

between them. Holy hot damn, he made it difficult to breathe. Or think.

It was easier when they didn't touch, but he was huge. Getting out of arm's reach would put her at a ridiculous distance and she didn't want to shout their business across the restaurant. Who knew how long the deck would remain quiet.

"Woman, what will it take for you to believe I don't know what happened to your brother?"

"Rye looking me in the eye and telling me that himself."

"You sent Judah out to my place already. They didn't find anything."

"You could have him somewhere else. You could have," she gulped, "buried or burned him."

"You shot at me and I welcomed you into my home. I tried to help you." He took a step closer, hands held out like he wasn't a threat.

She'd been fooled once before, though. She couldn't trust him. He'd already been caught in a lie. "Probably just some perverse reliving of your crime."

Ethan advanced on her again, a rumble trickling from his throat.

She shoved at him and he snatched up her wrists with one hand. He crowded her backward until her

133

shoulders hit a wall. He lifted her hands high above her head and caged her in with his body.

"Ethan." Tansey tugged but his grip remained firm. "Let me go."

Heat entered his eyes and she stilled. Ethan dragged one hand from her captive wrists down her arm and to her shoulder. His thumb and forefinger caught her chin. "These hands aren't capable of cold-blooded murder."

"I don't know that."

Ethan trailed a finger down her throat before planting his hand on her hip. His fingers massaged her through her clothes. "You do. Trust your instincts."

The air pressed down on her, trying to crush all her objections and wrap her in something else. Heat coiled tightly in her belly. Everywhere he touched sparked a fresh point of fire that burned through her defenses.

Insane. She was insane. The big cowboy topped her list of suspicious characters, and she was a damn puddle for him.

Ethan skimmed his nose up the column of her neck. His lips grazed over the shell of her ear. His breath tickled a tiny noise out of her chest.

"Believe me, Tansey. I'm not the culprit."

Instincts. Those were the ancient benefactors of survival. Ethan made hers go haywire. And trust? That was setting herself up for hurt. Trust was a commodity she lost long ago. No, she needed facts and proof. No sexy bear shifter would change her mind, no matter how close to taking that plunge she came.

Nothing made sense. Her reaction to him was off the charts. Her worry for Rye was a constant, ringing alarm. Viho wanted her dead, maybe. Her money, definitely. And Ethan was tied up in that, too.

Too much. It was all too much. She didn't have time to untangle any part of it or listen to the pounding of her heart triggered by the big man's touch.

Tansey lifted her chin and fought through the fog of desire. "Then find my brother and let him tell me that."

Ethan growled and left her on the deck alone.

CHAPTER 13

E than slammed the door of his truck closed and tossed his hat on the seat next to him. He needed a drink after all the bullshit. He couldn't head to The Roost because *she* could be there. One encounter was enough.

She'd ruined his entire day. His plan to stop for lunch then make a supply run dissolved into the desperate need to taste Tansey again. When she slammed the brakes on that idea—with the thickly sweet scent of arousal in his nose that she'd no doubt deny if he called her on it—he had to shift. Right then. He barely made it to his parked truck before his inner beast ripped out of him.

The push to be with her didn't end there. Oh, that'd be too simple. Manageable, even. No, his idiot bear tracked her from the shadows like some unrequited stalker.

His bear growled.

He didn't know why he was so bothered by her continued belief that he was some common criminal. He wanted to kiss the accusations from her mouth. Almost had.

He'd come so close to losing control on the deck. No one around. Her hands captured above her head. His good intentions drowned in her scent and only left wicked ideas.

For a distraction he didn't want or need, she sure kept digging under his skin.

Twin thuds jumped into the bed of his truck. He glanced in the rearview and found Hunter and Lorne staring back at him.

Well, at least Hunter wasn't going to get picked up for disorderly conduct in the middle of Bearden.

Ethan stuffed down the objections of his bear and made his way toward the only place that would do.

Defiant Dog sat on the edge of enclave and human territory. With the barrier active, he could take two steps from the old outhouse and feel the magic over his skin as he left his world behind and entered theirs.

Old, that. With shifters, vampires, and fae out in the open and enclaves revealing their locations, humans and their scientists descended on anything they could study. The Broken, the guardians of the enclave, were separated from the orbs that powered their magic. The barrier now only went up when one of the human researchers requested it.

Times changed, but Defiant Dog never did. Built into an old cattleman's hut on land no one wanted to claim, there was hardly room for two bottles of liquor, let alone the crowd The Roost drew inside town. Years of dirt and grime covered the floors and bar itself. Ethan doubted the grizzled old man behind the bar had washed a single rag that wiped out the shot glasses and pints crammed together on a teetering shelf behind him.

Ethan both loved and hated the place. It'd been his first drinking hole, and one where he regularly fetched his father. At that moment, the dive perfectly fit his mood.

A few faces lifted from tables in the dark corners, then went back to studying their drinks. The townies rarely ventured out this far. The ranchers drank too hard for them and no one ever called Bearden's finest to break up a brawl.

By the Broken, he hoped for a fight.

He sidled up to the bar and ignored his companions. Two fingers in the air summoned old Hector. "Whiskey," he ordered, knowing there was only ever one brand. He laid out the bills needed for the first round.

On cue, the three tapped their glasses and threw back their shots. Familiar warmth spread through Ethan's belly and he ordered two more before requesting a bottle of beer to nurse.

Hunter and Lorne stayed silent as they followed him to an open table in a dark corner. Ethan had appreciated it at first, but now it just grated on him. He didn't need babysitters, which was exactly what two pairs of quickly ducked eyes felt like.

He rolled his shoulders to relieve some of his tension. His muscles slackened, but the growling, restless unease stemming from his inner animal wouldn't disappear. Nothing would quiet the bear except the sendings he plastered all over Ethan's thoughts: Tansey.

He clenched his teeth to keep from shooting to his feet and chasing after the woman. "What are you two doing here?"

Hunter shrugged, not giving a shit about the infusion of dominance in the air. "You mean, why didn't I head into town and track down the cop Joyce is fucking?"

"Thought I'd have to alpha order you to bed like a child."

Hunter turned to Lorne. "He's going to make a wonderful father."

Lorne snorted, but the corners of his mouth twitched upward.

"What's that mean?"

"It means," Hunter sighed dramatically, "that I'm done chasing after Joyce. She wants to have a wild time, that's on her. Wish she was more honest about it with everyone, but it is what it is. And after watching you with Tansey, I know my girl is out there somewhere. I'm just waiting for her to show up."

Ethan scowled. "There's nothing happening there."

"After you didn't come back from the supply run, we called around," Lorne offered. "Even Hunter here didn't take long to figure out you had a run-in with that woman."

"Asshole." Hunter chuffed a laugh and punched Lorne on the shoulder.

Lorne punched him back. "Truth speaker."

Ethan shoved away and went straight for the bar.

Beer wasn't going to be enough to wash the taste of Tansey from his tongue or clear her from his mind. He returned with shot glasses and the whole damn bottle of whiskey. If he drank fast enough, maybe he could have a few uninterrupted hours of sleep before his system cleared and Tansey took back over.

His bear pouted in the corner of his head. Pouted! Like some puppy that'd been kicked. All over a girl that would just ruin their lives one way or another.

No, he was doing the right thing. The responsible thing. He needed to stay away from her addicting scent.

Hunter wasn't so easily put off. "You dropped everything for her. The only other person you'd do that for is Colette. Hell, the last time Alex and Lorne brawled hard enough to break something, you made them wait until the herd was shifted to a new pasture before setting their bones."

"There was a storm rolling in. They weren't going anywhere, but the bull was liable to run the cows into the hills," Ethan muttered.

"Point is, this stranger shows up and you can't help but get involved. That's the devotion I want someone to inspire in me, and Joyce just ain't her." Hunter downed the last of his bottle. "So, I'll wait."

"Be prepared for a long haul. Doubt there's anyone willing to put up with your sorry ass," Lorne teased on a quiet breath.

"Truth speaker," Ethan commended and poured him a shot while Hunter grimaced.

The smell of ripe fur and gasoline blasted through the swinging bar doors. Ethan lifted his nose and inhaled. "Something stinks like wet dog."

The quiet murmurings of the other patrons died down to nothing. Viho Valdana and two of his Vagabonds turned glowing eyes in his direction.

Yep. Those were his words tumbling out of his mouth. Fuck it. Asshole shouldn't have messed with his life. He shouldn't have taken a shot at Tansey.

Or at you, Tansey's voice shouted from the back of his mind. Even drunk and miles away, he had no peace from her.

Viho's lips lifted in a snarl. "The fuck you say, bear?"

"I said, who let that fucking wet dog stench in here?"

Next to him, Lorne groaned. Hunter grinned.

The wolves with Viho took two quick steps toward him and only stopped when Viho threw his arms wide. He issued quiet orders and the two fleabags crowded into a nearby table, eyes never leaving their alpha.

Viho sauntered over, each step rustling chains on his belt and vest like a damn biker symphony. He just needed coordinated engine revs and he could have his own show.

Ethan swallowed down another shot because clearly he hadn't had enough.

Flipping a chair around, Viho took a seat. He waggled a finger in Ethan's direction. "You and me, we have unfinished business. You stole my client."

"Client?" Ethan shrugged. "More like quick mark, eh?"

The Vagabonds were wanderers. Had been for years. Even so, they didn't need to stoop so low. They robbed and ran guns. If some of the rumors were believed, they were selling shifter blood, too, and leaving a trail of addicts in their wake.

Viho didn't know what it meant to be a good alpha. He controlled his people with an iron will, but he led them deeper and deeper into trouble. There was no surviving long-term on that. If some local cops didn't put a hole in him, someone within his own ranks would put him down.

He needed to get Tansey clear of the bastard.

Ethan blinked at the thought. She added a new

drive in his hatred for Viho. Viho was a danger and a threat because of their past. Women never factored into that. Until Tansey showed up on his land and made her demands.

Idiot inner bear. She wasn't their mate. He didn't want to shift his entire world around for her. His was fine without any extra problems.

"She was good money. Easy money. Couple of my boys had their eyes on her, too."

Ethan's hands tightened around his beer bottle. His bear rampaged through his head and flung images of Viho strung out and ripped to shreds to him. Tansey wasn't meant for the wolves!

A curious light entered Viho's eyes. "Guess I shouldn't expect anything else from Ashford scum. They're always taking what doesn't belong to them."

Ethan forced himself to relax and lean back in his seat. "And what belongs to you, Valdana? Way I remember it, your traitor father couldn't even find the balls for a proper challenge fight. Guess picking off cattle and duping humans is right up your alley, coward."

"I'll see you ruined. Stripped bare. Everything you ever cared about will wither and die. Who's going to take care of that sweet baby sister of yours when you lose everything?"

"Don't you threaten Colette," he warned with a growl.

"Oh, I'll treat her real nice, don't you worry." Viho grinned. "And the human, too."

A roar blasted out of his chest. Red haze filled his vision and he leaped to his feet. Those threats couldn't be allowed to exist. He'd force Viho to choke them back down with his own tongue.

Viho's backup came charging out of the shadows. Lorne and Hunter jumped up and cut them off. Ethan heard a crash of splintering wood right before Viho flung a fist at his face.

Years of waiting and frustration and betrayed hurt took hold. Ethan wanted to bleed Viho. All the pain of his family lay squarely at the feet of Viho's father. Instead of taking leave and making a place elsewhere, the fucker kept popping back up around Black Claw. Killing cows, watching from the woods, lurking, always lurking, and waiting for his moment.

Fuck that. Viho wouldn't take a damn thing that belonged to him. The ranch, his sister, his clan.

His mate.

No.

Yes.

Ethan threw a hard punch into Viho's stomach, then crashed his knee into the man's face as he stumbled. His bear snapped at his insides with the demand to be freed and have his own taste of wolf. Only the tight space kept the beast locked down.

Outside, though... Outside, they could rip and tear with abandon.

Viho jerked away, claws lengthening his finger-tips. A laugh bubbled out of his throat and showed off the blood coating his teeth.

Then he lunged, grabbing Ethan's arm and twisting them around and around while one tried to overpower the other. Ethan punched and clawed with the sharpened weapons of his own beast. Viho snapped. Chairs and tables and bottles were nothing but toys in their path of wreckage.

A series of blows shoved Ethan into the bar and Viho pounced. He wrapped his hands around Ethan's neck, cutting off his oxygen. A snarl gurgled at the back of his throat as his bear pressed forward.

Ethan reached for something, anything, and found a bottle of beer. He wrapped thick fingers around the neck and slammed it over Viho's head.

A sharp whistle and the cock of a rifle stilled their movement. The drip-drip-drip of blood and the panting of hard breaths were the only sounds in the tiny bar.

"Ain't neither of you worth the bullet." Hector

stared down the barrel at them, mouth drawn in a hard line. "Out."

Viho roughly released him, raised his hands, and took a step back.

Both sides separated under the watchful eye of Hector and his rifle. He didn't lower it as they were forced through the door with tails tucked between their legs.

Ethan straightened and glared hatred in Viho's direction. His bear still boiled with fury under his skin. The beast wanted to taste blood and the felt was unfinished. It wouldn't be finished until one of them lay lifeless in the dirt.

His land, his clan, his sister, his mate. Viho promised to see them all stripped away.

The line was drawn and crossed, the challenge made. Slinging himself onto the back of his motorcycle and roaring off into the night didn't stop the rage thrumming a deadly beat in Ethan or his bear from adding a matching snarl.

Viho Valdana wouldn't take one damn *thing* from him and live.

CHAPTER 14

E than squinted into the blinding sunlight and fought back a wave of nausea. His head pounded with enough force to split open. His joints throbbed. His throat and tongue were thick and dry.

Hangover, he told himself. He'd felt like shit all damn day and no amount of working his body eased the pounding in his skull. Too much whiskey topped by a shot of bloodlust would wreck any man.

His bear brushed fur against his mind. The beast sent another reminder of exactly what poisoned him, and it wasn't liquor. Their mate was out there, somewhere, and without protection. Viho could snatch her up at any moment while Ethan drove in the opposite direction.

He should have done more. Should have ended

the threat and risked Hector peppering him with bullets. Viho was out for blood. He'd had him in his grasp and watched the asshole ride away.

Ethan groaned and blinked away his double vision. What was done, was done. For the best, too. Tansey believed him to be guilty and he couldn't prove his innocence. All he could do was find a way to keep Viho away from her.

His physical reaction was more proof that she was pure trouble. He couldn't run a ranch and keep his clan in line if any disagreement sent him to his knees. He wouldn't last the calving season if he acted like an addict needing a fix. No. No mates. No biology driving him to set everything else aside. He had a job to do, and no pretty face would send him spiraling like his father.

His bear roared endlessly in his head. Sharp claws drove into his brain. Ethan welcomed them. Better the beast he knew how to manage than the shaky urges he didn't.

He tightened his hands around his steering wheel and turned down the road leading toward the lion pride's ranch. The large sign out front didn't even give a name for the property or the private drive. STAY AWAY, the sign ordered. Further down, another appeared. FUCK OFF.

Ethan shook his head at both and focused on the task at hand. He had to keep his shit together. Trent would sense any weakness. One threat was all he could manage. Two clans gunning for him would leave him outmatched.

Each bump in the road set his teeth on edge. His bear pushed harder against him as the scents of baked earth and big cats filtered through the windows. They were in the wrong territory. The snarling grew worse as the lion pride's barn appeared in the distance.

Ethan froze the second his boots touched the ground. He lifted his face and closed his eyes to better sift through the scents he drew deep into his lungs.

Faint, but there. Wolf. And not like any of the Valdanas that lurked on his land.

Jesse dropped to his feet from his truck and they exchanged a long look. At least he could trust his second not to make any stupid moves.

Trent poked his head out of his barn. "You here for my horses, Ashford?"

Ethan hated coming to Trent with his hands out. He was strapped for cash and bleeding money with every cow the Vagabonds picked off.

A good alpha did what was best for his people, he

told himself, so he grinned through the snarling of his bear and the pounding of his head. "Would I set foot on this barren wasteland otherwise, Crowley?"

"Wasteland, maybe. But we're far from barren. Got a few heavies ready to drop their calves soon and win us that prize money. How's your herd?"

"Asking so you can start putting the squeeze on your girls? Sounds like cheating to me."

"We'll see what the spring brings us." Trent cocked his head and sized him up.

"Calves and tourists, same as last year," Ethan answered.

Tension hung in the air between them. They were similarly sized. Even their animals were close in power. If the talk went down in flames, they'd have a brutal fight ahead of them.

Trent relaxed first. Jesse let out a breath behind him, as did the bachelor lions at Trent's back. One hurdle down, only a thousand more and a clan war to go.

At Trent's sharp whistle, his pride melted back into the barn and took Jesse with them.

The five horses were already draped with blankets and waiting to be loaded. There was some jostling with Trent's lions stepping on Jesse's toes, but sharp growls sorted out the hierarchy quickly.

Jesse looked each one over, rubbing a hand down necks and legs and checking alertness before leading them into the trailers. Any concerns needed to be raised before they left Trent's ranch.

Ethan folded his arms over his chest and turned to Trent. "You got a minute?"

Trent nodded and led him far enough away from the activity to make listening in difficult, but still kept them in sight.

"I couldn't help but catch a whiff of wolf when I pulled up."

Trent screwed up his face. Caution clung to him like a second skin. "There's a wolf," he said hesitantly. "Skittish fucker. I don't recommend anyone getting near."

"What's he look like?"

Trent waited a beat before answering. "Four legs and furry."

"You know what I mean," Ethan growled.

"Brown hair. Lanky. Wolf has a reddish coat." Trent sighed heavily and leaned against the fence post. "The man's not right in his head. He showed up here a few weeks back, spouting off about being hunted down."

Ethan stayed silent. A vortex of anger and sadness blasted off Trent. No wonder, really. He'd watched his entire family be butchered by hunters. If a shifter came to him with a story of being hunted, he'd be the first in line to offer them shelter.

"I put him up in a hut at the edge of the property. Far from you, far from anyone else. I don't even get near but once every few days to drop off some supplies. Even then, I stay well enough away." Trent dipped his chin to his chest and frowned. "You should, too."

Ethan's bear danced through his mind like some trained circus animal instead of acting like a proud apex predator.

Their mate asked for one thing, and they'd done it. This was their chance to prove their worth and earn her smiles.

Over the bear's celebration, the instinct to protect reared its head. Ethan didn't like what it meant for Tansey if her brother ran to the edges of enclave territory to hide.

If Trent's wolf was Rye. If. By the Broken, he could hardly contain his urge to move and prove it one way or the other.

Ethan ground his teeth together. Damn it all. The woman already changed too much.

"As much as I'd like to, I made a promise." He still saw the fire in her whiskey-brown eyes when he shut his own. Ethan shook himself and squinted at the lowering sun. Clouds gathered in the distance with the threat of an early spring storm. "When are you taking him supplies next?"

Another beat. Trent reluctantly answered, "Tomorrow."

"I'm coming with you."

Trent's expression hardened. "No."

"I need to. Finding this wolf might solve a lot of problems for the both of us." He squared up to the lion alpha. Didn't matter what Trent said next. He'd find the wolf himself if he had to. The easier path was one where he tagged along.

Trent rolled his shoulders. "Fine. I'll head out as soon as the morning mess is handled. I'm not waiting on you, so don't be late."

Ethan grinned. "Wouldn't dream of it. I'll get out of your hair until then."

"Bring your own damn horses, since you're taking all of mine," Trent called after him.

Ethan waved his agreement and caught up to Jesse leading the last horse toward the trailers. A peek into the larger hauler showed all the gear Trent was willing to send along neatly packed away.

"What was that about?" Jesse asked from inside the trailer. Quick work tied the horse in place. He dusted his hands on his jeans when he stepped back out.

"Once we get the horses settled at home, I need to head into town." Ethan continued at Jesse's questioning look. "That wolf we smelled might be the missing brother. She deserves to know."

Jesse toyed with a spare lead line. "You don't have to be the one to go. You don't even know if it's him."

"I don't want to spook him if there's a change in routine. Trent is taking supplies out tomorrow. I'll let her know. She might be useful for keeping him calm." Ethan shut the door and slid the bar locks into place. One trailer secured, they moved to the other.

"Or she could trigger something and set him off. We don't know why he cut contact and ran."

"Only way to find out is to ask." The sooner he could clear the wolf and the woman off his plate, the better. Viho needed all of his focus if the man amped up their fight.

Ethan's bear huffed and settled down. The aches and pains that troubled him all day faded into nothing. He prodded at the bear and tried to figure out the casual response to the potential threat.

The answer made him scowl.

Why fight? He was finally heading in the right direction—toward their mate.

CHAPTER 15

Tansey propped herself up on pillows and listened to rain patter gently against the window. Muriel said they were lucky it was just rain and not a late snow. Either were likely this time of year.

She browsed automatically, clicking from one tab to another for the billionth time. No new activity had registered on Rye's accounts.

Was it illegal? Probably. But with no one else looking and an entirely too-easy password to guess, she took it upon herself to dig for information in those first few days. Snooping every night quickly became a habit.

His phone hadn't been used since two days

before she started getting worried. The numbers he'd called or texted were to her, mostly. A few went to his boss at the bar he tended. He'd called his ex-girlfriend once, but she said it'd been nothing more than an accidental butt dial when Tansey pressed her for details. A second phone crossed Tansey's mind for a brief second before she dug into his bank account.

Her brother was broke. Dead broke. Ready to overdraft for buying a single stick of gum broke. No way was he able to afford even a shitty burner phone with the lack of money in his account.

Worry gnawed at her every time she saw Rye hadn't touched his phone or tried to withdraw the ten cents to his name. As much as she wanted to latch on to the idea that he was simply having a wild time as a brand new shifter, she couldn't believe it for more than a second. What had gone so wrong in his life that he left behind an empty bank account? He'd never hinted at any trouble. Then again, he'd never hinted that he'd disappear.

A sharp knock on her door pulled her from turning the puzzle pieces over and over. Anxiety threaded through her. She wasn't expecting anyone. Maybe Ethan was right, and Viho was outside her door ready to do away with her entirely.

Stupid. Viho seemed the type of man who knew how to dispose of a body. Taking her from her rented room was sure to blow back on him immediately. No, if Viho wanted her, he'd do it sneakily.

Judah? Muriel? Neither seemed likely.

Tansey pushed her laptop away and padded across the soft carpet to open her door an inch.

Six feet and more of delicious cowboy leaned against the wall across from her door. With one foot propped against the wall, thumbs hooked into his belt loops, and his hat hanging low and covering his face, he looked every inch of confident charm.

Tansey swung the door open further. Her eyes lingered over the bulging muscles of his arms and the hard lines of his stomach. Just the appearance of him kicked her heartbeat up a notch. Irritation, she told herself. Suspicion. Anything but good, old-fashioned lust.

"Didn't harass me enough, Ethan? You had to come back for more?"

"Well, if you're going to talk like that, I guess I'll take my information elsewhere." Ethan unfolded from the wall.

"What information?" Tansey asked at once.

He flashed a tiny smile. "I was at the lion pride's ranch on business and caught the scent of a wolf I didn't know. I pressed Trent for details and he admitted to letting a lone wolf stay on the edge of his land."

Tansey drew in a shuddering breath. Did the air rush out of the room all of a sudden? She felt as light as someone without gravity holding her down.

"Stay? Or *stay?*" The inflection made the two options very different.

"Stay. Trent said he talked about being hunted down. Do you know anything about that?"

She shook her head. "No. Like I said, I've been the only one trying to find him. Viho helped get me here, but something still put Rye into motion to begin with."

The information was something to add to the pile. Hunted down, he said. Maybe that fit with his empty bank account, but there'd hardly been any deposits since before he got himself turned into a shifter.

"Did he say anything else? What he looked like? Did he give a name?" she asked.

"Lanky guy with brown hair, is what I'm told. Wolf has a reddish coat. Does that sound like it might fit?"

The description wasn't much, but it was a start.

Rye was tall and thin. Dark hair most of the time. That combination fit more than a million people, she suspected. Combined with a red wolf cut down the numbers significantly.

"It's Rye. It has to be," she said with conviction. She raced into her room, then back into the hallway. "We have to go. It's him."

"Easy there." Ethan raised his hands. "It's night and it's raining. I could shift and maybe find him, but there's no way I'm taking you out. I won't risk you or a horse taking a fall and breaking a leg."

Begrudgingly, she stuffed her hands in her pockets. He was right. She had no idea where to go or what sort of terrain was out there.

"So when?"

She didn't like the image conjured up by her mind of Rye huddled in some leaky cave filled with bugs and snakes. Or the one of him crawling through the desert with dry, cracked lips. If Ethan wasn't rushing off for a rescue, then she trusted that Rye would survive the night.

"We'll head out in the morning. The way Trent tells it, the man might need some convincing we're not there to hurt him. Seems being untrusting runs in the family." Ethan shot her a pointed look.

Tansey turned on her megawatt, forced-to-be-polite customer service smile. "We call it being proactive."

Ethan snorted. "It's a pain for those of us on the other end."

For two solid heartbeats, she stared at him. He deserved an apology for the crap she'd thrown his way. She didn't even know where to begin. "Ethan, I—"

"Forget about it. I can't say I'd have done anything differently if my sister went missing," he said gruffly. "I'm glad this might be coming to an end for you. He's lucky to have someone so determined in his corner."

Emotions flooded through her as the reality set in. Tomorrow morning, it'd be over. She could ask Rye all the questions that'd piled up in her mind since he disappeared.

"Thank you!" She flung herself at Ethan, wrapping her arms around his neck. His hands snapped around her as he steadied himself against the surprise attack.

Then she felt him. *All* of him. And her mouth went dry.

A shiver worked through her at the press of his

body against hers. Hot, that was him. Heat rolled off him and settled deep in her core.

Her response had been much the same when he pinned her against the wall at the barbecue place. Or when he'd kissed her at the bar. She didn't know how he did it, or why she felt it the same since the first time his fingers brushed over her skin, but it was real. She didn't imagine the sharp reaction her body had for the shifter.

His lips had short-circuited all her thoughts quicker than the simple press of his palm against her arm. He'd known exactly how she needed to be kissed, teasing her into relinquishing control and showing her he knew what he was doing.

Another shiver worked through her at the unprompted memory of their kiss.

Was it wrong to want more?

Ethan's hands smoothed down her back and left a trail of fire in their wake. He came to a stop at her hips and slowly, carefully, peeled her away from him.

He passed a hand down his strained face. Silver replaced the blue of his eyes roving up and down her body. "I should go…" His throat bobbed with a hard swallow.

A growl filled the thick air between them. Ethan

swallowed that, too, then spun on his heel and stalked down the hallway.

"Hey!" Tansey called before he rounded the corner. Balls, she couldn't let him walk away like that.

Ethan stopped in his tracks. He didn't turn right away, which had her chewing on her lower lip. When he finally faced her way, he tipped his hat upward enough to show off those whirling silver-blue eyes that made her melt.

"I haven't eaten yet. Do you want to grab a bite? It's the least I can do—"

"After accusing me of abduction with a possible side of murder? After sending the cops to my ranch to toss the place? I'm still setting everything to rights after that one." Ethan's eyes danced with the teasing smile he barely kept off his lips.

"I was going to say after trying to shoot you, but I like those better. Less violent on my end." Tansey calmed the butterflies in her stomach. "For all the help you've provided when I didn't deserve any of it, can I buy you dinner?"

"My mother would roll over in her grave if I accepted. How about I take you out instead?"

He'd convinced her once before to celebrate a win, and that was simply getting her information in front of the right people. A real, solid location on Rye's whereabouts was an even bigger reason to honor the occasion.

"All right," she said with a look thrown over her shoulder as she stepped back into her room to grab her wallet and phone. "But only because you're buying."

CHAPTER 16

Tansey rushed through the door of the bar with Ethan close behind her. His palm hadn't left her lower back since he whipped open the door of his truck and guided her across the puddle-filled parking lot. She ignored the disappointment when he snatched his hand away.

Leah toddled from one end of the bar to the other, hand on her belly when she wasn't reaching for discarded glasses and bottles and passing over replacements. A dark-haired man tending the bar with her turned some dials on a machine and cranked up the volume on a fast-paced country tune. The crowd responded with a cheer and couples stepped into motion.

Tansey wiped at the raindrops clinging to her

skin. The slow rainfall that'd wet the night when they left Muriel's had turned into a downpour while they stuffed themselves full of barbecue.

"Claim us a seat," Ethan said over the noise. "I think there's a spot near the pool tables that just opened up. Stout's your poison, right?"

That he remembered surprised her. Then again, the entire evening was a surprise. After butting heads at every step, the last thing she expected was for Ethan to show up at her door to announce he might have found her brother. He could have easily passed along the information to the police and left her out of the loop.

"That's it," she told him. He tipped his hat and made his way between packed bodies while she squeezed through the press to find them a table.

She tried not to let the fact that he remembered her drink count for anything. Dinner had been pleasant and thawed the tension between them. They'd talked about plans for the next day and how he got tangled up in her mess, but he stopped her before she could make any big apologies. The chivalrous cowboy showed himself with a tip of his hat, a slow smile, and an insistence that he help a woman in need and buy her dinner after.

He'd kept his paws to himself and maintained his

polite exterior. She knew something wilder lurked underneath the pleasantries. She'd seen his eyes churn with hunger and heard the deep gravel in his voice. She'd also felt her heart tripping in thrilled reply.

He was a confusing contradiction and her response to him was equally stumping. The smart thing to do, the right thing, was to keep far away from the man. She'd been so hell-bent on finding her brother that she didn't care what damage her accusations may have caused. Trust, too, should have been out the window. Instead, she felt compelled to believe his words and her body craved his touch.

Pinned down. Bundled up. Pressed against a wall. She was intimately familiar with the strength the man possessed. She'd experienced the toe-curling kiss he could deliver. Was it so wrong to want another taste? She pressed her thighs together to ease the ache those thoughts spawned.

Tansey jumped as a dark pint slid across the table. Ethan squeezed himself into the empty seat and took a sip from his own bottle. His nostrils flared and his eyes dropped to her chest, then jerked back to her face.

He couldn't *smell* her, could he? She wracked her brain for every tidbit of information she knew about shifter senses and decided, probably, yeah. Warmth spread across her cheeks, but she didn't drop her gaze.

A coy smirk lifted one corner of Ethan's mouth and he took another long draw, saying nothing. He didn't need to. He set his hat on the table and mussed his sandy hair into model perfection.

Yep, it'd be a miracle if she didn't throw herself at him before the night ended.

The pool table next to them cleared in a rough jostle of motion and curses. Ethan knew the group, giving them tight smiles as they passed by. He jerked his chin toward the empty space. "Have you played before?"

Tansey ducked her face to hide her smile. "It's been a while."

A month, in fact. Rye taught her years ago and they played on slow nights when she visited him in their hometown. Without him, she only passed by tables while trying to corral Viho in an effort to get him to work.

"Come on." Ethan stood. "I'll teach you."

Score. Maybe she could make some extra cash and take back a little control. Ethan tipped her off balance too much.

After racking the balls and chalking the cue

sticks, he crooked a finger for her to join him. Tansey reached for the cue he offered her, but wasn't prepared for what came next.

He stepped behind her, bending them over in the process. He covered her hands with his and positioned them on the cue. If it weren't for all the noise and chaos of the bar around them, her thoughts would have slipped into what other fun could be had in the position. Even so, her skin prickled at the warmth behind her and her stomach tightened.

"It's like shooting a gun," he said against the shell of her ear. "You know how to do that already."

Tansey glared over her shoulder. His eyes laughed at her. And her body heated another ten degrees.

"Take a breath and line up your shot. Draw back." Ethan eased her into the movement. "Exhale and shoot."

It was just the first shot, so she landed her hit off center and sent the ball flying to split the rack. Colors tumbled in all directions, but none made it into a pocket. Perfect.

"Your turn," she said brightly and glanced over her shoulder again.

Ethan's eyes dropped to her lips and he hesitated a moment before stepping away. He stayed silent through his turn, eyebrows drawn together and a heaviness around him.

Tansey didn't know what to make of the critical gaze that watched her line up her shot and once again miss hitting anything of use. Blue and silver swirled together into the mixture that was quickly becoming her favorite color.

Ethan seemed to find an answer and nodded to himself, then stepped around the table to find his spot. Just as he bent into position, he raised an eyebrow. "There's something I just can't quite wrap my head around. How is it that you were the one to track down your brother?"

"What do you mean? Wouldn't you do everything in your power to find your sister?" She chose her next spot of attack at the far end of the table.

"Yeah, but you have other family, don't you? A man back wherever you come from?"

"A man?" she asked flatly. Her eyebrows shot up and her jaw tightened. "You think I need *a man* to tell me where and what I can do?"

"Never mind." Ethan smirked around his beer bottle. "I get it now."

"What's that supposed to mean?" Eyes narrowing, she paused before taking another shot.

His smirk didn't falter. "I meant no offense.

You're clearly a strong, capable woman. Some men might find that intimidating."

More than some. She was too self-sufficient. They didn't feel needed. The complaint was a common one when the men of her life inevitably departed for greener pastures. But why was she supposed to pretend at weakness for someone with one foot out the door?

Tansey grimaced and sank a ball into a pocket. Ethan scratched at his stubbled chin and fixed her with an unreadable expression. Damn. She was supposed to be playing poorly this round.

"Our mother wasn't very happy when Rye went furry and holds the opinion that he's out howling at the moon." Tansey tucked her hair behind her ears, suddenly feeling a little self-conscious and irritated. At her mother not giving a shit and everyone else unwilling to help. At herself for having no one else to rely on. "And I've been on a lot of last dates," she admitted in a rush.

His throat bobbed with a hard swallow. "They can't have all been bad."

She ticked off her fingers while Ethan took his turn. "There was the one time I was invited on a group outing, and he tried to fob me off on his brother, who took one look and asked what he'd get paid. Another time where I was supposed to meet him for dinner, and found him at the tail end of a date with one of my friends. Oh, you'll like this one. I catered an event at a country club and met a guy. A couple weeks later, he rescinds an invitation to a different event at the same club because he didn't want to be seen with the help."

By the end of her litany, he stared and shook his head in silent commiseration. Not willing to end there, she took him through a second category of greatest hits.

"Those are just the biggest w-t-f moments of my long-term relationships. I could tell you about the first-last dates, too. Like the guy who showed up and asked if we could eat and drink with horse masks on, the one who told me to go wipe off my makeup because the lipstick was the same shade as his ex's, or the one who insisted that my shellfish allergy was fake and slipped some clams into my meal when I went to the bathroom. Joke's on him, I threw up on the armrest on the way home. Hope he had fun cleaning between his seats."

"You did that on purpose, didn't you?"

She feigned innocence. "Rude. I would never act so maliciously."

"He deserved it," Ethan chuckled.

The rich notes echoed through her like a chord strummed to life. For a split second, she thought warmth and awareness flared to life in the exact center of her heart. But that was silly. She couldn't think of him as anything more than a friend. One she recently tried to interrogate and have arrested, but a man who still came to her when he stumbled on the information she sought. Nothing else existed between her and Ethan.

He tapped her hand resting on the table and brought her attention right back to him. "You know what your problem is?"

Tansey motioned for him to give up his words. The earliest memory she had of her father was him sniping to her mother about opinions being like assholes; everyone had them and most of them stank. "Here we go. Let's hear it."

"You choose the people who won't be a challenge." He laughed at her scoff and eye roll. "I'm serious. You squared up to me, ready to throw down to get answers about your brother. That takes balls. You know what I hear when you tell me about these boys? They couldn't handle you."

"That's ridiculous. I don't want to be alone for the rest of my life."

"So find someone that challenges you. Do you

want the guy who hands you to his brother? The one who is seeing someone behind your back? Or do you want to be the one they drop everything for?"

Like he'd done for her?

Tansey shook her head to clear the stray thought. Impossible when his hand pressed against her lower back as he edged behind her and to his drink.

Suddenly parched, Tansey followed suit. The air between them felt as thick as ever, pressing them closer. Part of her resisted. Another part, the selfish side she rarely let out, wanted to give in.

Find someone who challenged her? Ethan had done little else since she put herself in his path. He clashed with her, tempted her, and drove her crazy in the space of a day. Every moment they spent together built up more electricity than she knew what to do with, or could even guess how it would discharge.

She knew the moment the game was up. Ethan's eyebrow drew together and his eyes bounced around the remaining balls. Suspicion and a little bit of humor tightened his features when he turned to her.

"You've done this before."

"What? You've never been hustled?" Tansey dragged a finger down his jaw as she swished past him to take her shot. "Don't let a pretty face distract you."

"Well played, Nichols. Well played," he said in a gravelly voice. His eyes didn't leave her for a moment, blue swirling into bright silver. "You're not anything like what I expected."

Tansey fluttered her eyelashes to hide her sudden pleasure at his compliment. "Don't go falling in love with me, Ashford. Apparently, I'll demand all your time."

"You're safe," he said flatly. "No mates for me. I have my hands full already."

"With your ranch and lending helping hands to anyone who waves a gun in your face?" She missed and cursed under her breath. "Does your sister listen when you hand out all the good life advice?"

"Colette?" Ethan snorted. "Colette doesn't listen to anything I say. She's a lot like you, actually."

"Tell me about her."

A small smile lifted his lips. "Colette's studying for a degree in agricultural science, maybe wants to spin that into being a vet for large animals. She has this idea about coming back home and helping out here, but I don't want that for her."

"No family business, then? No Ashford dynasty extending through the ages?" Tansey wrapped her fingers around the cue stick and leaned against the table next to Ethan.

His expression shuttered. "No. No dynasty. That's asking to have your life burned to the ground. It's just us trying to make it from one year to the next."

That sounded heartbreakingly familiar. Pinning her future to a hope and a dream never worked out.

"Were you very young when you started caring for her?"

"About thirteen." He leaned against the pool table next to her. "I used to take her out with me when I'd do chores. I remember one summer, she couldn't have been more than six or seven, I found her swimming in one of the cattle troughs. She said she didn't need to go to the lake when we had pools at home."

There it was again. That deep, tricky feeling of longing for something more spiked as he talked about his sister. He had a family he could rely on, and that depended on him. Not just blood, either. The other shifters of his clan were under the umbrella of his care. She wanted to belong to something more than just herself.

Tansey sighed and leaned her head against his shoulder.

Too late, she realized what she'd done.

A low growl vibrated in Ethan's chest. He wrapped his arm around her waist and spun her into him. She stood between his legs, hands splayed across his firm chest, lips inches from each other.

Tansey leaned back. Her fingers stroked against his chest of their own accord. Bright blue eyes swam into focus, the heat and intensity residing there stealing her breath away.

The moment stretched on. They were caught in their own tiny bubble and the rest of the world slipped away.

"What are we doing?" she whispered.

This version of Ethan was different from the confident cowboy flashing a bright smile, or the one that filled the air with the tension he carried, or the man willing to get into a fist fight for her. The Ethan holding her steady by the hips was untamed charisma. Enticing. Sensual.

"You told me to find your brother," he said in a low voice.

Tansey swallowed hard. A challenge and a promise-keeper, that was Ethan. "And you did."

A crack of thunder overhead preceded the sudden blackout. Haunted howls sparked a ghoulish cacophony in a truly juvenile fashion.

"Five minutes!" Leah shouted. "If we don't have lights by then, you're all kicked out!"

A swirl of air was her only warning that Ethan leaned closer. The darkness cloaked him and gave her no clue where he'd touch.

She shouldn't have wondered.

Ethan growled, the words indistinguishable to her human ears, then crashed his lips against hers. Tansey gasped and he took advantage of the moment to seal them together in another world-tilting, mind-altering kiss. His mouth moved firmly over hers, tongue tangling and tempting her as surely as the needy snarls that rumbled in his chest. Savage, sexy man.

The lights were still out when Ethan eased back from their kiss. He didn't let her have a moment to think. His hands closed over her shoulders and his mouth dropped to the crook of her neck. "I don't want to wait around. Do you?"

Tingles raised the fine hairs up and down her body. She slowly shook her head. Could he see it in the darkness? She needed two tries to find her voice. "Where do you say we go?"

"I'd never let a woman walk herself home."

CHAPTER 17

Don't fall in love.

The words stuck to the back of his mind since she spoke them. Teasing, like fifty percent of the words that fell from her lips, but they wouldn't leave Ethan alone.

Too bad his bear decided that was out the window the first time he caught Tansey's honeyed scent. Then she'd held her ground and twisted him into knots at every turn. The bear was ass over snout for her.

He wasn't much better.

Don't fall in love.

Tansey stumbled through her door at the inn and rounded on him. Wet strands of hair clung to her face and neck from their run between the parking lot and building. Her chest heaved with big breaths, but nothing in her scent or eyes said she was scared. Hungry, that's what they were. Those whiskey-brown orbs of color demanded he finish what he started at the bar.

Ethan advanced on her, slamming the door shut behind him in his haste to get to her. He was so fucking glad she had a room at Muriel's. He wouldn't have been able to wait the entire drive back to Black Claw and he wanted to take his time. Taste all of her. Build up her moans before he even unzipped his jeans. He would have fucked her hard in his truck, too, but this would be so much better.

He cupped her cheeks, angling her face for him to devour her lips. He couldn't stop tasting her. She was like a meal he'd been starved for his entire life. Now that he had her, he wanted to savor her and inhale her equally.

This wasn't love, he told himself. This was infatuation. Hot, dirty, need to feel her break all around him infatuation.

His bear snarled at him and Tansey pulled away.

She ran her fingers lightly over his lips. "Was that…?"

"My bear." He swallowed hard. Would she run?

Sour her sweet scent with fear? He tried to shove his bear to the back corner of his mind. "Yes."

She leaned forward and nipped his lower lip. "Don't you hide him from me," she ordered.

"Good girl," Ethan growled. In a flash, he snaked an arm under her ass and hauled her up. Tansey automatically wrapped her legs around his waist and smoothed her hands against his chest. *Yes,* he wanted to purr. *Touch me.*

The fearlessness she showed at every turn demanded his attention. She wasn't one to back down from anything. By the Broken, she spent the last month with an entire wolf pack in her determination to find her brother. That was the hard core of steel he needed in a mate. She wouldn't run scared from the wildness at his center.

Mate? No. He might have defended her against Viho, maybe let himself think it was true for a flash of a second, but she couldn't be. He didn't have a mate waiting for him. He couldn't.

His protests grew weaker with each utterance.

His bear swiped at him, then turned sweet as pie for the hot little piece in his arms.

Colette would have laughed at him. His sister wasn't scared to stand up to anyone. She would have looked him in the eye and asked if he was an alpha of his own clan and ready to take what he wanted, or a boy scared to repeat the mistakes of the past.

He was not his father. He'd never leave his people to flounder without him. He had skin in the game to make them work, make them better. The time spent with Tansey was proof he could balance his life and hers. He'd been useless without her, wondering if she was in danger and who he'd have to rip apart if she got hurt.

So, what did he want?

Tansey. He wanted Tansey. Her nails digging into his shoulders, her hot mouth trailing kisses down his neck, her arousal filling his nose... She wanted him, too.

With their massive misunderstandings out of the way, it wasn't hard to picture her at his side. They had a lead. They'd set aside their issues and gotten in sync. That was what it meant to have a mate, wasn't it? Working together instead of in opposition.

Tansey groaned and Ethan echoed the sound. He reached the bed and let her slide out of his arms. Her hands shoved under his shirt and pushed until he reached behind his back and hauled the wet fabric off his body.

The AC kicked on and scattered goose bumps over her damp flesh. Her discomfort wasn't allowed.

Ethan grabbed the hem of her shirt and peeled it off her body. Black lace clung to her frame and Ethan groaned. Perfect, just fucking perfect. His cock pressed painfully against his jeans at the sight of her luscious curves. She wasn't coy, either, and didn't try to hide behind her hands. She knew exactly the effect she had on him.

Tansey reached forward, one arm wrapping around his neck. Her other hand closed over his shaft, squeezing and rubbing him through his jeans.

Ethan growled. In one motion, he had her flat on her back. A tiny, shocked breath left her lungs. Her eyes snapped open and focused on him. He tested the air; no fear. The sweet scent of her arousal made his mouth water.

He leaned back and allowed himself a moment to admire her and get a grip on himself. His balls ached with the pressure the sight of her built in him. He thought he'd have a heart attack if he had to spend another minute not inside of her heat.

He kissed a path over the swell of her breasts. Her nipples peaked under the fabric and begged for his attention. He bit through the lace, teeth softly closing around the bud. He ran his palm up her ribs and closed around her neglected breast. He lapped and sucked until her breaths came in needy pants and she arched her back to give him more.

More. He wanted everything she'd give him. He wanted to taste every inch of her before the night was over.

Then he wanted to do it all over again. His bear rumbled a lifetime of agreements.

Don't fall in love.

Fuck, but the feisty woman had dragged him halfway down the path already.

He slammed the brakes on that thought. She had her own life and family. Her own dreams. Just because she was unlucky in love and tangled up in her brother's problems didn't mean she was ready to throw everything away. She could skip town as soon as her brother was found.

Infatuation. Lust. One night, maybe a handful, of feeling her shatter around him. That was all he could allow himself to grasp at, no matter how she looked with her hands twisted into his hair and back bowed in a silent plea for more.

His bear railed against the thought of letting her go.

Ethan eased her zipper down and pressed a small kiss to her navel. Another to the waist of the panties he exposed. More to her generous thighs, her knees, her calves. The tops of her feet each received pecks before he switched his path back to her center.

"Fuck, sweetheart," he groaned. "I can't wait to taste you."

Her eyelids fluttered open, eyes dark with lust. Even so, she batted his hands away from the waist of her panties. "No one really wants to do that."

"Mmm." The noise vibrated in his chest as he eased her panties down her legs. She looked gorgeous with her cheeks already flushed. "You've been with boys."

She huffed a laugh, eyes rolling at his comment. "And you're the real man to show me what I need?"

He spread her legs open and licked into her. The shock of it slammed her thighs closed around his head and she arched her back. He growled, long and low, and pushed her legs back open.

"Sweetheart, your body was made for pleasure. Let me prove it to you."

Her mouth dropped open and Ethan inwardly grinned. Stealing her words and leaving her speech-less felt like a victory.

One to be outdone.

He ran his tongue up her slit and nearly lost his fight not to plunge into her on the first roll of her hips. Slow. Controlled. He ran his tongue up her folds again and again, hitting her clit at the top of each stroke. He focused on wringing pleasure from her body and proving himself against the line of weak boys in her past.

He held her spread open for his taking, hands wrapped around her thighs to keep her from retreating. His, that's what she was in that moment. Needy groans and clenched hands were all for him.

Her thighs trembled. His bear shoved forward and demanded he finish the job, claim what belonged to them. Ethan kicked the beast back before his fangs could lower. Marking her wasn't his intention. Licking her until she thrashed and moaned was his goal.

He swiped his tongue through her slick, wet heat. "Look at me," he groaned. "Want to watch you come."

By the Broken. Whiskey-brown eyes landed on him.

"Good girl." He slid his tongue deep inside her.

Her mouth dropped open in a perfect little o. The noise the poured out from her lips was pure ecstasy. Her hands tightened in his hair as he bobbed between her legs, working with the jerks of her hips guiding him to the rhythm she needed. Sexy woman.

Perfect woman. He would be a fool to never slide between her legs.

And those shining, hungry, beautiful eyes never left his face. Not until her head fell back and her thighs clenched down on his ears.

"Ethan," she moaned, lost in her release.

Ethan ripped his jeans down his legs as fast as he could manage, then he joined Tansey on the bed. Her legs fell open for him and he rubbed his cock up and down her wet heat.

"Do you want this?" he purred in her ear. The tease was as much to hear her acknowledgment as to give him a second. His bear clawed at him again with more demands to bind the woman to them.

Not now.

Not yet.

Not when he didn't know what the future held and she had no idea the pull she had over him.

One night, or a lifetime, Tansey had him by the balls.

"Quit teasing." Her teeth nipped at his neck as a shudder rolled through her body. "Need you now."

TANSEY WAS LOST. Ethan's taste. His strength. The

deep, husky, pleased noises he made as he slowly slid his impressive length into her, inch by glorious inch. Good lord, he smelled good. Forest and dirt and sweat. Had anything ever been so intoxicating? All of it worked together to fog her head up with never wanting the night to end.

She tried to replay the whirlwind of events over and find out where she'd let her guard down. That first kiss? When she'd shuddered at being captured so easily against a wall? No, tonight, when he'd snuck past her defenses and given her a glimpse of what it would mean to have Ethan on her side.

They'd found a tentative trust when she had no reason to hope for it. This man, for whatever reason, took up her cause. Hers. That was an important distinction. He sought her out and gave her hope about her missing brother instead of hunting down Viho and getting any type of revenge.

She wanted loyalty. The bone-deep kind she wanted to give to someone else. Ethan was slowly, strangely, earning it.

He propped himself on his elbows, arms shaking with the effort not to plow into her like those stupid boys he was so damned concerned about. Not that he had anything to worry about. None of them had treated her like a buffet made solely for his tongue, or groaned about it through the first taste to the last.

Strain cut sharp lines across his strong jaw as he bottomed out inside her. His eyes whirled with blue and silver. "Fuck, Tansey," he growled through gritted teeth.

Strength stared back at her. Loyalty. Mischief. He was a tough man with a spine of steel. He had to be, to grow up with so much weighing on his shoulders. Ethan Ashford was a good man.

She could almost trick herself into thinking he could be her good man. She was halfway there. The wishing stage was just as dangerous as the believing.

Don't fall in love, she told him. A joke, then. A warning, now.

Tansey pulled him down and licked his lower lip. "What did I say about teasing?"

He released a tight breath. His eyes flickered, then he slanted his mouth over hers in a blistering kiss.

Tansey gasped into his mouth as his hips retreated, then slammed back inside her.

Her legs trembled as she wrapped them around him. She needed the extra leverage, needed to ground herself against something or risk spinning entirely out of control. Ethan was the rock she needed while the rest of the world slipped entirely away.

He worked her body relentlessly. Teasing play was long gone and a feral need had awoken in them both. His arm curled under her and gripped her shoulder, holding her steady as he pounded into her slick heat.

Nerves sparked with each hard thrust. It was hard to breathe with the air so thick around him. Like molasses. Just as tempting, too.

Tansey stifled a moan, teeth grazing against Ethan's shoulder. The hoarse groan he made in response fried her thoughts as he thrust faster, harder.

Her skin tingled with fire while her mind, somewhere distant, recognized what he'd done to her. Ethan dragged her closer, dug deep into her, and branded a part of himself on her. Every second teetered her further over the edge.

"Ethan," she panted.

His name was the only word she could manage. She needed more. Needed to feel all of him with every last bit of restraint stripped away.

Tansey dragged her nails down Ethan's back. He reared back with a roar, eyes burning silver, and pushed to his knees. His fingers dug into her hips and hauled her into place.

"Fuck," she moaned. Stars burst behind her eyelids at the feel of him in an entirely new position. He utterly filled her.

His thumb swept across her clit. "Come."

The words were all harsh order and inhuman growl. They drew a shudder of pleasure from her very middle.

"Come now," Ethan commanded again. "Want to feel you on my cock."

His eyes alone would have done the trick. The dirty words were like a flick of a switch.

She cried out as she crested, riding the wave of pleasure he demanded from her. Every muscle reacted at once, tightening and pulsing with her release.

His roar vibrated through her as his cock throbbed inside her. His movement stuttered, then stopped, then picked up again as he dragged every twitching sensation out as long as possible.

Ethan collapsed on top of her. He rolled to the side and tucked her against him, one leg thrown possessively over her and an arm locking her to him. He became a blanket, which she thought should irritate her instead of giving her comfort.

His breath sighed against the back of her neck and she froze. This was it. The moment where he cuddled only because it was expected of him. He'd slip away as soon as possible.

Ethan brushed his fingers lightly up and down her arm and made no signs of moving.

"Ethan?" she whispered into the darkness after a long moment.

"Hm?"

"Why does the air get... heavy around you sometimes?"

His fingers trailing over her skin stopped. "It's because I'm dominant. My bear is pushing for obedience."

Tansey rolled over to face him. A wicked smile lifted her lips as she crawled her fingers up his chest. "So you don't like to be challenged?"

"Careful, sweetheart. I might just have to show you who's in charge."

In a quick move, she had him on his back. Feeling crazed and hopped up on lust and curiosity, she leaned down and scraped her teeth over his flat, brown nipple. His hands slapped down on her hips and dragged her against his growing shaft.

"You can try," she dared.

CHAPTER 18

"You ready for this?" Ethan asked. Four pairs of eyes watched them from the porch, summoned by the sound of his truck bumping up the driveway.

Tansey stifled a yawn. Bags lined her eyes, but she looked at him with clear focus. She hadn't uttered one word of complaint since his alarm pulled them from exhausted sleep an hour earlier. That earned his respect as much as the eyebrow she arched in the direction of his clan.

"As long as they have coffee, I'm ready for anything." She swiveled her head and threw him a wry smile. "They look so cute lined up and waiting for daddy to get home."

Ethan choked on his laugh. "I'll let you be the one to tell them that."

He stepped out of his truck and into the asscrack of dawn to the sounds of whoops and whistles. Ethan ducked his head in quiet male pride that surged at the memory of his night with Tansey. His bear was absolutely pleased to have his scent all over the curvy woman. That lingering odor of possessiveness was the only thing that kept the beast caged beneath his skin.

"Classy," she muttered without a hint of annoyance. She beamed a smile in their direction and raised both middle fingers in an early morning salute that had them doubled over with laughter.

"You left classy behind at least eight miles ago. I'd say we're lucky these ones are even housebroken, but I'm not sure about Alex."

Alex straightened with a scowl. Ethan cut him off before he could let loose any of the wild curses that were never far from erupting out of his mouth. "Don't you slackers have work to be doing?"

Jesse crossed his arms over his chest. "We were wondering if we needed to send out a search party."

"Why?" Tansey interjected. "Afraid I ate him alive?"

"Other way around, more like it," Ethan muttered

for her ears and caught an elbow in the side. Smirks from the others said he hadn't been quiet enough. Whatever. He was a damn adult and no prude.

"They're just lucky I let you out of bed," she sniped back. "Would they have been able to tell one end of the horse from the other if I hadn't?"

Hunter's eyes danced with his broad grin. He wagged a finger at Tansey. "Oh, this one is funny. I like her. Can we keep her, boss?"

Ethan growled low in his throat. He needed them gone before he started staking his claim with claws and fangs. "Head on over. I'll catch up in a second."

Snippets from the muttering males reached his ears and were immediately discarded.

He grabbed Tansey's hand and spun her into his chest. Her hands flattened against his chest as she turned laughing whiskey-brown eyes on him.

Heat crawled down his spine and settled at the base with just that little contact. Before he could help himself, Ethan leaned down and sipped at her lips. "Listen, Trent won't be ready to head out for another couple hours..."

Tansey contracted and expanded her fingers, almost like a cat kneading him. "That's fine. You take care of what's needed."

The words were different than the only other

morning she'd been on his ranch. She'd been full of demands and questions then, and couldn't wait to get on the move. Hope reared its head on the vague possibility of her understanding the work that went into his daily life.

He dipped his face again and caught her in another kiss. Tansey just... melted against him. Her lips parted without prompting and he swept his tongue inside.

By the Broken, he couldn't get enough of her. The soft sounds she made, the feel of her skin, everything. She made him want to spend the day in bed and forget the world existed. His bear rumbled agreement, with the added demands to sink his fangs into her skin and bind her forever.

With a strangled groan, Ethan tore himself away and spun her back out with a tiny swat on the ass. "Head inside and help yourself to some coffee. I'll be back soon."

The walk from house to barn was short, but he took his time. He needed the coolness of the early morning to calm his raging blood. His bear wanted him to turn back around and nuzzle up behind his mate. The human half wanted to, as well, but at least put more stock in one head than the other. Duty called. He'd had all night to avoid it.

Renewed whistles and wolf howls greeted him the moment he stepped out of the darkness and into the warm glow of the barn doors. All except Alex stopped what they were doing to clap loudly and offer him a shit-eating grin.

"Look who finally has a walk of shame," Hunter called out.

Ethan pointed at him. "At least mine isn't actually shameful."

Alex twisted up his mouth in something between a snarl and a pout. "She's not going to come in here and change everything up, is she?"

Lorne grunted. "My only hope is this stops your dick hanging out all the time."

"If that's what it takes, I'll mate the next woman I see," Jesse added.

The jokes underscored the problem at the heart of his clan. They were misfits. Hunter had a past he was running from. Alex and Lorne, too, if he widened his definition by a fingernail. Jesse kept his shit together mostly through making sure the others didn't tear each other apart. And him? Well, he didn't want distractions taking him away from maintaining their balance. He was responsible for all of them.

"Nothing is changing," Ethan reassured his bears.

Except for spending the night away from the

ranch. He couldn't remember the last time he'd done that without the involvement of too much liquor and the bars of the police station.

"Besides," he cleared his throat to hide the sudden longing that filled the pit of his stomach, "there's no telling what will happen after today. She might take the brother and head back home."

That wiped the grins off their faces. Even Alex's grumpy doubts were replaced with something close to concern.

His bear clawed at his middle and roared loud enough to make his ears ring in protest of losing their mate.

"Anything happen last night?" he asked before anyone said a damn thing.

Jesse shook his head. "Nothing. No big bad wolves huffing or puffing all night."

Surprising, that. And a relief. Guilt over leaving his clan and ranch undefended grated on him. Tansey was a distraction he wanted to find a place for in his world.

"We'll keep a watch. I doubt Viho has gone far. Seems he wants to put up a fight, so we'll give him one if it comes to that," he said gruffly. He'd better be dead if the wolves took up on his territory. "Have the new mounts settled in?"

The question brought them back to their tasks. They had work to do. Cows to tend, horses to mind, their bank accounts to watch. They fell quickly into their routine of running the ranch. He counted it as a win that Hunter cursed out Jesse only once and Alex didn't shift and brawl.

About an hour after the sun fully popped over the horizon, a piercing clang jerked Ethan to attention. "What in the hell?"

A quick glance at Lorne showed the man throwing more hay to the noisy cows heavy with calves. He shook his head in bewilderment.

Hunter raised his head from changing the tire on one of the horse trailers. "Is that a chime?"

Ethan stomped around the barn with the others in tow. Tansey stood on the porch of his home and clanged the triangle chime again.

"Better come now if you want your food to stay warm!" she shouted.

As baffled as the others, Ethan shrugged and made his way toward the house.

The scent of breakfast made his mouth water even before he pushed through the side door. Tansey moved from one end of the kitchen to the other, arranging plates and checking on cooking dishes. She tossed him a huge smile and dipped back to rummage through the fridge for whatever she needed.

He rubbed at his nose. If he wasn't struck dumb by everything else, he thought she smelled pleased. His bear liked watching her work.

"What's this?"

"I found the bell wedged in a junk drawer. Which, by the way, your organization in here is abysmal. Nothing is where it should be. Why are the pans way over on that side when they'd be more useful by the stove?"

"And the food?"

She passed by him on the way to check a sizzling pan of bacon and planted a quick kiss on the cheek. "This is my way of saying thanks. I told you I'd make you a meal as payment for helping me. This isn't dinner, but it's something."

Ethan was buffeted by the others streaming in behind him. They practically drooled while they added piles of food to their plates and took a seat or dug in where they stood. Their groans were in solid agreement that whatever she'd cooked up was better than their usual fare.

Tansey lorded over the entire scene. She smacked a dish rag at Lorne for trying to sneak more bacon from the strips still sizzling away on the stove, then slid a fresh batch of scrambled eggs on a plate and shoved them at him instead.

The sight and smells hit Ethan smack in the chest with the full weight of longing for something more than his bachelor lifestyle.

She looked perfect in his kitchen, feeding his males. That caregiver streak that sent her running with a wolf pack to hunt for her brother was evident in the piles of food she prepped for them all.

His mother used to do the same for his father's clan.

He couldn't get attached. Not before he could see her clear of any blowback from Viho and certainly not before he knew what she planned once she had her brother back in her life. She'd stormed into his life with fire in her eyes and he didn't know if he'd still stand if she blew right back out.

"I'm saddling up two horses after breakfast," he said. "Not sure how long we'll be gone. I want to keep the herd close and extra eyes on the heavies until we return."

Nods all around took his orders in stride. They knew what went unspoken. Wolves could be lurking and waiting for an opportunity. Keeping everyone rounded up helped their chances if it came to a fight.

Jesse wiped his mouth with a napkin and globbed

a spoonful of hash browns onto his plate. "Have you ever been on a horse before, Tansey?"

"I took a few lessons as a kid. It's like riding a bike, isn't it? You do it once, it's not so difficult the next time."

Lorne snorted into his coffee. Jesse fought to keep the smile off his face. Hunter and Alex looked at one another, then nearly collapsed into laughter.

Ethan wiped his own grin off his face. He didn't want to threaten the food about to get dumped on his plate.

Hunter reached for a piece of bacon. His lips still twitched at the corners, but he managed to sound bored. "Lady, anytime we hear one of you say 'lessons,' it's always those fancy saddles and riding around in circles. We don't do that crap here. This is real riding."

Ethan winked. "Don't worry. I'll take care of you tonight." He leaned in closer and nipped at her earlobe. He dragged her scent into his nose. "Draw you a hot bath and rub down all those sore muscles."

The others whistled and banged fists on countertops.

Tansey waved the spatula in his face. "It can't be that bad. Just watch. I'll be fine."

His bear clawed for control, which Ethan denied.

The beast wanted to protect her from any sense of danger or hint of pain. Taking her to Trent's territory put her in the crosshairs of angry lions or deranged wolves.

Leaving her behind would be worse. No, he needed to keep her close. He wouldn't trust anyone else to keep her safe even if she agreed to stay behind. He wouldn't trust her to sit still, either. Last thing he needed was her sneaking across onto pride lands and sparking a war between his clan and Trent's.

"Out of sheer stubbornness, you just might be."

CHAPTER 19

"What is *she* doing here?"

Tansey ground her teeth together at the sheer animosity in the man's voice. A deep whisper in the back of her head wanted to slide back into the truck and lock the doors.

She folded her arms over her chest and stared the man down. She didn't back down when Viho or his Vagabonds started blustering. This man wouldn't see her retreat, either.

"Trent, Tansey. This might be your wolf's sister," Ethan explained. "She might keep him from doing anything skittish."

"Or might make him wild if he perceives a threat. Of all the ignorant bullshit you could have pulled—"

"It's done. She's here. She's going with us."

The air felt heavy as neither man blinked. Dominance, Ethan explained to her. She'd put good money on them being equally matched in a fight.

Whatever silent conversation existed between them ended as Trent spun away abruptly and stomped toward the barn. "She's not my damn problem. I'm not babysitting a fucking human."

"That went well," Tansey said lightly.

"Told you Trent wasn't a fan of humans," Ethan answered as he undid the latch on the trailer and unloaded first one horse, then another. "This is Jolie. She should be sweet enough for an inexp—for your first time out here."

Tansey ignored the slight and stroked a hand down the mare's tan neck. Her legs and tail and mane were a richer brown. "What's your's named?"

"Patches," Ethan grunted. He fixed her with a stern look. "Not my choice. Colette started calling him that when he was just a foal. Poor guy never stood a chance at a decent, manly name."

"Something strong, like JD or Remington, I imagine."

"Fine names, both of those. Patches would have done them equally proud."

"Hm." Tansey nodded to herself. "I think I know

the real reason why you want your sister to stay away."

"You don't mess with the naming of a man's horse." Even though he griped, his mouth hitched up in a simmering smile.

The relaxed, joking Ethan snapped to attention as soon as Trent led a horse into the sunlight. Four pairs of glowing eyes watched from the shadowed barn entrance.

The lion shifter flicked a dismissive glance at her, then focused on Ethan. "It's about an hour rough terrain from here."

"Won't be a problem."

"And I'm taking supplies in case he doesn't want anything to do with you."

"Smart move," Ethan agreed pleasantly.

Trent glowered at her for a long moment, then swung into his saddle with a mouthful of muttered curses. Ethan shrugged, then helped her up and adjusted her stirrups.

As soon as Ethan mounted his horse, Trent twitched his reins and took the lead. Tansey followed with Ethan behind her. No one said a word, which left her all alone in her thoughts. Two men fought for focus in her mind, and she didn't want to share the nerves either sparked with Trent. Ethan, Rye. Rye, Ethan. Better to let everything go blank than work herself up into something that couldn't be solved in the saddle.

The uncomfortable silence and intruding thoughts were shoved aside for the scenery. The land was beginning to come alive, but still had a way to go. Patches of new green grass mingled with the old growth the snow recently unveiled.

In the distance, snow still clung to the peaks and some lower ridges. Closer to their little party, a few mountains looked like they'd been sheared away with steep cuts down to the hills below. Other areas were gradual slopes into rolling foothills. Regardless, bright blue skies cut above the land with barely a dot of cloud in the distance.

"You're staring," Ethan interrupted. He pressed his heels to his horse and pulled up next to her.

"I never stopped to get a good look at places, I guess. This is the furthest I've been from Minnesota, but I was so focused on finding Rye that I didn't see anything except the road ahead of me." Not that there was much time for sightseeing. Her time was spent attempting to pester Viho into action and trying to earn any side cash she could.

"And now?"

Her gaze bounced over the mountains that hid

Bearden and the ones further in the distance. Cows mooed in the field they passed while a big bull watched over them in silence. Her skin tingled with the potential she felt from the land readying for new life and the hope of being reunited with her brother.

She didn't know how to put any of that into words that wouldn't make her sound like a crazy person.

"It's not at all what I expected." Truth. None of it fit into the story she planned for herself, especially not the bear shifter cowboy at her side.

"They don't call this Big Sky Country for no reason." Ethan jerked his chin in one direction. "It's a bit flatter out east. We built in the mountains to give us more protection. At least that's what they said in school."

Shifter school, in a shifter town. She felt like a child when it came to the other world. She had to learn, though. For Rye.

And Ethan, a tiny voice whispered in the back of her head.

She shoved the thought to the side. He was a confirmed bachelor and didn't see a future with a mate. Their little dalliance was just that, and nothing more.

Tansey swirled a finger through the air. "This was all hidden away?"

"Yep. The roads leading in and out of the enclave would make humans feel unwelcome if they edged too close. If they persisted, all they would see was wilderness. The higher ups in town did their best to keep anything developing where it'd give us away."

"It's like something out of a horror movie," she teased. "Let me guess, there were watchers on the roads, too?"

Trent glared over his shoulder. "Didn't do a damn lick of good. Might have saved us all a heap of trouble."

"Locals were paid to watch the roads and discourage traffic. Some of us had to be extra careful. My land has a spit on the other side of the barrier—when it's active—so the clan has to be kept on a tight leash near the border."

"Could be tighter. Could be more discrete," Trent muttered.

Tansey was sure it was exactly loud enough for her to hear. She didn't know how or why Rye would have chosen the surly lion to help hide him away. The man seemed to go out of his way to be unwelcoming.

Ethan scowled in his direction. "Problem, lion?"

"You wanted to give her a tour ride, you should have done it on your own time. She don't need to know our secrets."

"*She* is in this life whether you approve or not," Tansey said through gritted teeth. "My brother is the one we're trying to find."

Trent grunted and fell back into uncomfortable silence.

Not soon enough, the hut came into view. Unpainted, worn wood looked sturdy enough, even if the entire thing leaned a little too much to one side. A pipe rose from the more even half of the building, but no smoke curled out of it.

Come out, Rye. Please, come out. Wolf or man, just please come out.

"This is where you stashed my brother?"

"It's sound enough. Bed and a stove do in a pinch. He wasn't exactly looking for company."

The defense sounded distracted to even her human ears and when she quirked an eyebrow at Ethan, she found him looking away into the distance. "What's wrong?"

Trent dropped to the ground. He scooped up a handful of dirt and sniffed it, then let the grains fall through his fingers. His nostrils flared when he lifted his nose into the air. "The scent is faint. He's gone."

Her stomach sank. So close. So fucking close, and Rye still slipped through her fingers. She was no closer to understanding why he left in the first place or how he ended up in a shack in the middle of nowhere Montana. "How long?"

"Days, maybe. Spread out. Let's see if we can pick it up."

The last was meant for Ethan, and Tansey watched as they cut lines away from her. Trent led his horse on foot. His mouth opened and closed as he gulped down big breaths.

Ethan stayed in his saddle. His eyebrows furrowed as he watched the ground on either side of his horse.

Not knowing what else to do, Tansey dropped to the ground and started making her way toward the hut. The shifters could track from the outside, but maybe Rye left something behind indoors.

Gunshots fired in quick succession, ringing across the range before she even recognized the noise. Bullets zipped into the ground next to her horse and at her feet.

Ethan jumped from his saddle and flung her behind him. "In the hut. Now!"

Tansey didn't think twice. Another burst of gunfire followed her across the tiny yard and she dove for the hut door.

A lone howl rose eerily in the distance, growing the pit in her stomach and sending chills down her spine. Others picked up the cry and answered. Through the slats of the hut, she watched the pack stream down from their hidden spots and gather in front of the two men. Coats of all colors rose along arched backs.

There was no warning before a lion burst out of Trent. His mane shook with the huge roar he yelled at the invading wolves. Fangs longer than her hand were exposed in continued snarls as he paced back and forth in front of the hut.

But it was the giant bear that held her attention. Ethan's silver eyes churned with fury. Huge claws dug into the earth with each step he took toward the biggest wolf at the center.

The wolves jumped for the bear, piling on the unfairness. A small number teased and chased the lion, but it was clear the bear was their target. It was like watching a nature show in action, with creatures that shouldn't have brawled together. The wolves wanted to cut the bear away from all hope of pooling the fight with the lion.

Both bear and lion ripped and tore into any target they could find, but the wolves made up in speed and numbers what they lost in sheer mass. They jumped in and out of fang or claw range, then nipped at the ass ends, sending Ethan and Trent spinning round and round as they unleashed fury where they could reach. Blood dripped from black fur and tan coat and colored the ground red.

A whicker to her left drew her attention. Eyes rolling to show their whites and reins dangling in the sand, all three horses clustered together at the edge of the hut.

Tansey threw the door open and rushed straight for Patches. She wouldn't ever forgive herself if she let those two men go down without any help. She'd be damned if she let the wolf pack tear her apart without taking a chance to save her skin.

She ripped the rifle from the saddle, pulled the bolt, and fired at the nearest wolf without hesitation. The wolf slowed his attack, then fell into the dirt.

One down, but there were still so many. Ethan whipped one from his side, and two more jumped for him. She didn't dare try shooting any from his back, and they all seemed determined to land there.

A growl from her left sent her swinging the rifle. She fired just as the wolf leaped for her, catching the creature in the side. The beast yelped with pain and stayed grounded, but didn't stop his advance.

Ethan roared, shaking and clawing the wolves still clamoring up his back and sides and ran straight for her.

Her hands shook as she worked the bolt. Fear doused everything but determination. Each growling step the wolf took forced her back another. Then another. Her palms slick with sweat, Tansey lifted the rifle. She refused to go down easy.

Then the bear was there, crowding between her and the wolf. He swiped huge paws and snapped his jaws over the wolf's back. The beast scrambled for release, but Ethan shook him and threw him to the feet of the others still hungry for blood.

Whatever the wolves saw in Ethan's silver eyes made them turn and run.

Tansey's heart thumped once. Twice. Then strong arms wrapped around her and crushed her into a solid wall of muscled chest.

"Are you okay? Did any of them bite you?" Ethan's words fired from his lips.

"I'm fine. I'm fine." Everything shook and it took her a moment to realize it was her. From head to toe, she quaked. Fear, adrenaline, she wasn't sure which was more powerful at that moment.

Ethan kept her locked to his chest as he threw open some hidden bag on Patches' saddle. He angrily stuffed his legs into a fresh pair of jeans, then locked her tight against him once again before rounding on Trent.

"The fuck did you do?" Ethan snarled. He pressed a balled up shirt to his side to stem the flow of blood. Even as she watched, the shallower cuts closed. The deeper ones would take longer, and probably be gone by morning.

The lion shimmered until a naked man stood in his place. He cocked his hands on his hips and bared his teeth. "Me? You're the one that brought the human. Bet she was the one that lured them here. Who else knew we'd be out here? Can't trust a human."

Tansey pushed away from Ethan, anger burning away her shock of a real shifter fight. She wagged her finger in Trent's face. "You were the one who told Ethan about the lone wolf you had hidden away! How do we know it wasn't you who set us up? What the fuck did you do with my brother?"

He spat on the ground. "Like I'd deal with the fucking Valdanas. They aren't my problem. Talk to your man about their kind."

Two lions appeared in the distance, hauling

themselves at a pace that must have been faster than their natural kin. They skidded to a stop right in front of their alpha, snarls lifting their lips.

"Run the fences! Put down any wolf you find," Trent roared. He whipped back around, blackness tipping the finger he pointed in their direction. "Get that fucking human off my land, Ashford!"

Ethan tugged her toward the horses, but Tansey jerked out of his grasp. "He doesn't mean Rye, does he?"

"Tansey, let's go."

"No! Not if he means Rye. Stop him!"

"Tansey, listen to me." Ethan spun her into his grasp, stooping to catch her eyes. "Rye is gone. His scent is so faint that I don't think he's been here for days."

"But he was here. He could still be around somewhere." She would not cry. Not now. Not in front of that infernal man.

"He's not now and we need to leave. We've worn out our welcome." He hugged her tightly again. "I promise I will do whatever it takes to find him."

CHAPTER 20

Tansey sighed and let her head fall forward while Ethan rubbed her shoulders and down her back. True to his word, he'd drawn her a bath in a large, claw foot tub after a quiet dinner alone. Also true: everything hurt. Her thighs and calves ached, and even her stomach and sides felt the workout of a fight for her life and a hard ride home. The hot water and Ethan's nimble fingers did the trick for her sore muscles, but did little for the pain in her heart.

So close, and the mystery Rye saddled on her still remained unsolved. She didn't even know for sure if he'd been the one hiding out in the secluded hut. She was no closer to finding her answers than the day she stepped onto Black Claw Ranch.

Worse yet, she'd come far too close to savagery. She didn't want to imagine what would have happened if Ethan and Trent were just a touch slower, or if the Vagabonds had more numbers on their side. Maybe the big wolf would have landed fangs in her skin and her mother would have two furry children to disapprove of instead of just one.

"Tansey," Ethan rumbled softly and drew her back to reality, "I think it's time to consider Rye is caught up in Viho's business."

Water sloshed as she folded her knees to her chest. "I know. I just don't understand why."

She still couldn't piece together the connections or why Rye would even go near the man. What hurt even more was the idea that the two were alike, but Rye never showed her that side of himself. When had they gone from close siblings to strangers? A shiver worked its way out of her frozen center. If she couldn't depend on her own brother, then she could count on exactly no one.

Ethan cupped a hand of water and let it trickle down her back. "Sometimes I don't think it's our place to understand. We clean up the messes and find a way to keep living."

"I feel like I've been cleaning up messes my entire life."

"The right person will appreciate that you care enough to help others when they need it." He swiped a finger through the water before she could object. "This is getting too cold. Pull the plug and I'll get you a towel."

Water swirled in a violent cyclone down the drain. Tansey wished it would suck down all her worries with it.

Ethan wrapped a large towel around her body, then surprised her when he caught her under her knees and carried her into the bedroom. He settled her against a pile of pillows and pulled her legs across his lap.

The pressure of his fingers on her calves held off the questions building inside her all afternoon and into the evening. She'd stayed silent on the ride back, sensing Ethan needed to piece himself back from protective beast to protective man. The others felt it, too, when they finally arrived back at Black Claw. They made themselves scarce while the dark cloud hung over Ethan's head. The shadows had slowly fizzled out, and the last of his intense and gloomy anger slipped down the drain.

She needed to dig, though. Any piece of the puzzle might be the clue she needed to figure out

Rye. "What did Trent mean about the Vagabonds? You've been vague on Viho's connection to you."

"That is an old, unhappy story." He paused in his massage.

"Seems to be the only type in the world these days."

Ethan settled on the bed next to her. He propped a hand behind his neck and frowned at the ceiling for a long, quiet moment. Sadness colored his tone when he finally began to speak. "Viho's father was part of my father's pack. They were old friends, as far as I know, and the Valdanas were the first to clan up with my dad. They had some hard years, and some good. Found mates, added others to the clan. Something changed somewhere down the line, though I was too young to really see what was happening. It's so obvious now that I look back on it. Tension within the clan was tearing them apart, but rather than step up and make a challenge for alpha, Viho's father worked the shadows and kept everyone snapping at one another."

"That's not all, is it?" she asked when he paused. The air thickened around her. Not the usual heaviness she when he went dominant. This was heavy with emotion.

His throat bobbed with a hard swallow. Sightless

eyes still faced off against the ceiling and the memories playing through his mind. "I remember it like it was yesterday. The screams. The howls. It was only a couple weeks after my thirteenth birthday when tensions boiled over and lines were drawn. Colette was just a toddler. Mom rushed into my room and ordered me to watch Colette, and hide if anyone but her or Dad came back to the house. Then she ran into the night. That was the last time I saw her alive."

Grief flared in his eyes, all trace of wild silver gone and replaced by clear, pained blue. Tansey snuggled against his chest and wrapped her arm tightly around him. There was nothing she could say to erase the past hurts. She could only help hold him together in the present.

"By the end, we were the only ones left," he continued. "Dad burned them all, pulling those that remained loyal apart from the ones that followed the Valdanas. By rights, he could have left them to rot. He took me to the side and explained why he wouldn't do that. They were still his clan, even if they chose the wrong side.

"After, he sat in his room and poured drink after drink. Then he stopped pouring and went straight for the bottle. You see, when an alpha loses someone, they feel that bond snap back into them. He lost his entire clan in a matter of hours. I think we're responsible for keeping Defiant Dog open all these years." He huffed a mirthless laugh.

"You were so young. To take that all on yourself..." Tansey grimaced. At least her remaining parent did her best. Ethan's hardly seemed to try at all.

Ethan cleared his throat. A shrug tried to play off the mountain he was forced to shoulder. "Someone had to work. At first, Dad hired someone to help. Then we couldn't afford that, or they didn't want to deal with him. So I started working. I barely finished school. Jesse came over as much as he could, which was often. His old man wasn't any better than mine. He fixed up one of the huts and moved in by the time he was eighteen. He was always going to be my second, and we've collected our strays ever since."

He swiveled his head and cocked an eyebrow at her. "That's all to say I didn't even know Viho was alive until a few years ago. He rode in with his Vagabonds and kicked up a fit. Got himself banned from the enclave, which is a feat. He makes appearances every now and again, but never gunned for me so hard."

Tansey rolled to her belly and propped her chin on her fists. Other than Rye having some connection to Viho, she couldn't see how her brother fit in with Ethan's tale. He'd given her another dead end, and a peek at what made him tick. "So, here we are. The cleaners and the survivors. For the million dollar question—how do you plan to spend your future?"

Ethan waved a hand across the blank board of his destiny. "Anything to keep it going. We're barely squeaking by as it is. Viho killing off my herd isn't helping. This place is in my blood. It's the only thing I know. I have to keep Black Claw running."

"What about opening up for extended stays? You already have the trail ride business set up. The others have their own little places to sleep. There are all those rooms just waiting to be filled upstairs. Offer a bed-and-breakfast with real ranch experience. Make your guests muck out a stall or three." She'd joked before about his potential clientele looking for flirtations with the past. Fixing his problems was a distraction from her own. The house had good bones and he'd kept up on repairs, as far as she could tell. For someone looking to monetize his land, the idea seemed like the logical next step.

"I'd need someone to run that. I can't keep the clan in line and the tourists unmaimed and fed. Unless you have someone in mind?" Ethan dragged her down and smirked against her lips. "I kind of like the idea of banging the boss."

Heat flushed her cheeks. "I wasn't talking about me, in particular. It's just an idea to consider."

The laughter died in his eyes. In a flash, he had her hands pinned above her head and stretched her out beneath him, caging her with his body. His fingers pinched her chin and forced her to meet his gaze. "Don't shut down like that. Don't erect all those walls. You know more about me than I've probably told anyone else. Say what you want."

She wanted… so many things. Her life back to normal, but that looked increasingly unlikely. In her new reality, one where she let a shifter and a cowboy care for her after a physically and emotionally exhausting day, she wanted someone like him. He wasn't a boy who'd shy away from the tough events; Ethan was a man who'd face off against adversity and rise to the top. He was someone who would stick around.

"I want to see where this goes," she said on a rushed breath. "And not just because I'm talking you into my dream job. You said to find someone that challenges me. You get my back up every other thing that comes out of your mouth and tangle me in knots every third. You're interesting, Ethan. I don't think there's a single man like you in the world."

"Well, now, that's just mathematically impossible. There has to be at least one other workaholic with a desire to prove himself against his flawed father's memory." He tightened his hand around her wrists before she could snatch one away, and pinned her knee down when she wiggled for a jab. At his mercy, he leaned in and sipped her lips. "You're interesting, too, Tansey. Halfway insane—and that's a generous estimate—and a caregiver at heart. Just promise me you won't go challenging any more wolves with only a rifle as your defense."

"I will make sure there's a giant bear ready to back me up." She'd never forget the power unleashed by the big beast, nor the instant turning from his own survival to her protection.

"You couldn't pay me enough to fight all the battles you manage to create." The second slow taste of her lips said the opposite.

Her heart got stuck in her throat, but she managed to find the words. "Now that's too bad. I think we make a great rivalry."

Ethan flashed her a wicked smile before his lips pressed against hers. He laved his tongue against the seam and delved into her mouth as soon as she opened for him. Slowly, he kissed her, but there was nothing chaste or sweet about it. He was pure fire and she couldn't get enough of his heat.

He tugged at the knot holding her towel together and laid her bare. Bright blue eyes devoured her from her head to her toes, and back again. He lingered on the space between her legs on the second pass, tongue darting out to lick his lips.

Her nipples tightened and a wave of liquid heat rushed through her at his obvious desire. What woman wouldn't want that? To be wanted and cherished by a ripped cowboy with an animal under his skin ticked all the boxes from sweet to sexy and everything in between.

Emboldened by the look, Tansey butterflied her knees open.

"Fuck," Ethan groaned.

Tansey gave him a wide-eyed and innocent look as she skimmed her hand down her soft stomach and to her slick entrance.

"You're killing me," he said, voice turned to deep gravel.

He wasn't the only one about to die. Her head swam with what he did to her and what she still wanted. Desire percolated through her entire body and made her feel like she'd explode. "You're over-dressed."

He sat up on his knees and ripped his shirt off, then fell back over her. He pressed his mouth to the base of her throat. "You're so fucking beautiful," he growled.

Ethan dragged his fingertips down her ribs and to her hip. He squeezed her there just as his mouth crashed against hers again. Slow, steady strokes of his tongue and rolls of his hips gave her a preview of what came next.

When his fingers reached her knee, he reversed course. Up and up, his touch blazed against her skin. He pushed between them and gripped her breast hard. Tansey moaned and arched into his touch, and Ethan gave her more. Fingers rolled and brushed over her nipple until she rocked against him to ease the ache between her legs.

"Ethan," she gasped. "Please."

Sexy, teasing man grinned against her lips. He grabbed her wrist and dragged her hand to the waist of his jeans, then kissed her senseless again.

She popped the button. A tiny noise lodged itself in the back of her throat when she felt nothing but skin underneath. She closed her hand around his thick shaft and squeezed on the next jerk of his hips, relishing in his sexy snarl.

Ethan shucked his jeans faster than she could track. Blue eyes stared at her when he returned. No hint of silver existed in them when he leaned over her. That sent a shiver down Tansey's spine. He felt more real, more present, than ever before.

He felt important.

His fingers twined with hers and lifted her hand over her head. Gentle man, sexy man, and still in charge.

The head of his cock teased her entrance with feather light brushes against her folds. She chased the touch, rocked her hips to encourage him into more, but he held her steady. His lips kissed her forehead, her eyes, her cheeks. He dotted her neck and shoulders.

Only when he sipped at her lips did he roll his hips forward and sink into her. He eased back, watching her face as he did it again. Still bright blue, still entirely Ethan.

Tansey fluttered her eyes closed at how good he felt. That loss of one sense only increased all the others. Ethan's breath in her ear tickled her nerves. The feel of him moving inside her spiraled pleasure through her. Heat, impossible heat, blazed off him and ignited something in her heart she wasn't prepared to consider.

Her teeth caught hold of her bottom lip, loving everything he did to her.

Pressure built inside her as his pace kicked up. His hips bucked faster into her, meeting her and moving with her. His fingers tightened on hers, still holding her hand above her head. Her soft cries twined with his sexier growls.

"Look at me," he ground out.

The order was nearly the same as one he'd given before. And yes, her body reacted with a tensing of muscles and simmer of pleasure.

But his eyes... They were telling her so much more. Promises were held deep in the blue orbs that watched her spiral apart. She could have all the time she needed to see what had sparked between them and he'd go the distance at her side. This wasn't a tipsy tryst after a night of celebrating. He made promises to her body and committed to divining out that hazy, possible future ahead of them.

"Ethan," she gasped.

"Fuck, sweetheart." He quickened the pace, abs flexing with each hard thrust. His growl was near constant now, sawing in and out of him and vibrating through her, and when he lay a hard, sucking kiss on her shoulder, she was lost.

Ecstasy pulsed through her, and Ethan wasn't far behind. He locked them together as deep as could be and throbbed warmth into her. They moved together, lazily drawing every aftershock from each other and slowly sinking back into reality.

Ethan cupped her cheeks and murmured against her lips. "You're mine, Tansey."

A happy hum vibrated in her throat and she nodded. Maybe neither of them could believe it fully or admit anything else, but they were tied up too much to ever let go.

Instead of frightening her, she held on for dear life.

CHAPTER 21

E than stroked a hand over Tansey's dark hair and enjoyed the silence in his den. His bear didn't roar at him and his own thoughts didn't spin through the worry cycle that kept him restless most nights. He simply held the woman who had vastly complicated his world.

He didn't want to let go.

Tansey wanted to see what was growing between them, but Ethan knew. He'd denied it from the moment he caught her scent. She'd wormed her way under his skin and into his heart. His bear wanted to keep her.

Bite. Mark.

Mate.

She shifted in her sleep and dragged her hand

over his stomach. His skin warmed at the touch and his heart swelled.

Complicated woman. Insane woman. Caring. Gorgeous.

His.

She wanted time? Perfect. He needed time to set his world to rights. That time would be used to make sure no wolf ever cornered her again. He made his promise to find her brother, and he'd do that, too.

Then they'd get down to business. He had his goals and she had her ideas. Maybe it wasn't weakness to let someone in. Risky, yes. But better than going it alone. Maybe together they could fix up the ranch and run it the way it should be run.

Rooms to be filled, she said. His bear rolled on his back like some happy puppy. He certainly had some ideas of how to fill those rooms, and none of them involved letting anyone into his territory.

Ethan tightened his grip on Tansey. He saw both the good of a mate and the bad when she no longer existed. The threat of the bad kept him afraid of repeating his father's mistakes when he should have eyeballed the good. Colette and himself came from that pairing. They had their entire futures ahead of them. They owed it to themselves to live it to the fullest instead of staying wary of the past.

Tansey was his future.

Faint noises of activity intruded on his quiet contentment.

"Get Ethan. Now!"

Eyebrows shooting together, Ethan eased out from underneath Tansey as boots pounded up the front porch and through the door.

"Ethan!" Lorne shouted. "Fire!"

Ethan's blood froze as he stuffed his legs into jeans. Fire was an enemy in the best of times. Lives could be lost in a flash.

"What's happening?" Tansey murmured. Hair twisted and sticking up in all directions, she looked exactly like the chaos that ruled his life.

"Don't know. Stay here. Stay safe. I'll be back when I can," he answered, already at the door. He tugged a shirt on as he hurried out.

He met Lorne halfway through the house and followed fast on the man's heels as he turned and darted back through the front door. The sight outside nearly stopped his heart. Nausea swam his vision and sank his stomach.

Flames burst through the roof of his barn. Inner beams glowed in stark contrast against the night. Orange tendrils licked against the walls that had stood sturdy from the day his father erected them.

In the red glow, cattle huddled at the far side of their paddock and bleated their fear. The rest of his clan scrambled to hook hoses to anything with a water flow. Steady streams sprayed in a losing battle.

"Where'd it start?" Ethan roared, striding toward the burning building.

"Upper levels. Something sparked in the loft and it spread fast. I already called it in." Hunter's eyes were wide and wild with his inner beast. His fists opened and closed in agitation. "I don't know how they got the jump on me—"

No question who he meant. He couldn't smell any scents over the burning wood and straw, but there was only one pack of wolves looking to destroy him. Fucking Viho.

And fuck him, too. He let that pretty face in his bed distract him. He should have hunted down the Valdanas the moment they crossed the line from casual stalking to full threats. His entire clan should have gone after the wolves right along with Trent's lions. He should have been on watch. He should have expected something.

Ethan quashed the litany and self-recriminations. Tansey wasn't the problem. Viho didn't deserve a moment of his thoughts right then.

"No time for that. Get the heavies out of the

paddock and into the main herd. We'll cut them back later." If they survived the night. "Help the others get hoses on the flames."

Inside, horses screamed in terror. They weren't just his livelihood; they were his responsibility. No creature deserved such a slow and painful death as being trapped inside a burning barn.

"Soak me down," he ordered as he stared at the flames. "Then get ready to corral the horses when they come rushing out."

Ethan dug a bandana out from his pocket and tied it over his face. He held his arms out wide and didn't flinch when the chilled water hit his skin. As soon as he was wet from top to bottom, he ran for the barn doors.

Smoke hazed the air and made the shadows cast by bright, angry flames all the eerier. Overhead, fire crackled as it ate through straw and wood and everything it touched. One of the cross beams looked like the red-hot top of a matchstick, and sparks rained down on the ground.

Ethan crouched low, trying to keep out of the danger as much as possible as he made his way to the first occupied stall.

Patches reared and kicked at the door. Jolie, across the breezeway, blew panicked breaths and spun around in quick circles. All down the line, horses made their terror of the heat and flames known.

It'd take too much time to dodge flailing limbs to punch open the doors leading to the paddock outside. Ethan unlatched Patches' stall and waved for the horse to make his way toward freedom. Better to send them fleeing into the night than have no mounts in the morning.

Jolie followed quickly, then two more. He worked down the line, zigzagging across the breezeway as fast as he could. The fiery beam always got a glance as he crossed.

Ethan sent another horse running for the doors with a smack on the rump. One more. One last horse to set free.

Above him, the beam cracked. Ethan tucked and rolled just as the wood split down the middle. Burning pieces of roofing fell with it, igniting the straw left inside the empty stalls.

Ethan coughed his way to the last horse. Smoke rose from the bottom of the stall from embers catching fire. The mare—one of Trent's—spun and lashed out with her back legs, but neither doors nor wall would give.

He glanced over his shoulder. Too much fire and

debris. He wouldn't willingly go through that hell himself, much less make a poor animal run the obstacles.

Ethan waited until she turned her head back his way, then unlatched the door and grabbed her halter. He held tightly and pulled her into a tight spin to reach the outer door.

Then they were in the night. Red still glowed and smoke still thickened the air, but the heat of the barn inside was washed away by cool spring air. Ethan spluttered and ripped the bandana away from his face to suck down a clean breath. The mare tossed her head, but he kept a tight grip on her until he could send her through the pasture gate with the rest of his herd.

Wailing sirens and flashing lights roared up his drive. Too late for his barn, but at least the animals were alive.

CHAPTER 22

Tansey dragged on clothes and raced to the window, phone already pressed to her ear to summon the fire department. She twitched aside the curtains and watched the horror unfold on the other side.

Glowing orange and red served as a backdrop to illuminate the shadowy figures scrambling around the barn. Hoses and buckets were pulled from thin air, but the water barely put a dent in the burning wood.

The screams were the worst. Cows trapped in the pasture nearby and horses still inside the stalls cried out for a desperate rescue.

Her stomach turned at the overwhelming sounds

and the terrible sights, but she couldn't look away. Wouldn't.

The burning barn was on her. She got involved with Viho. She led him straight to Ethan. The problems that existed between the two were only exasperated by her. Right or wrong, she chose Ethan over Viho. To Viho, she was just one more possession stolen by the Ashford clan.

If she'd just stayed in Minnesota… If she'd never found her way to Bearden, to Black Claw…

Doubts tumbled end over end in her mind while she watched the clan struggle to salvage their barn and business. She was the match, the catalyst, that sparked those deadly flames.

After what felt like an eternity, a dispatcher answered and promised help was on the way.

It'd be too late, she realized. She wasn't the only one with the thought. Cold washed over her when she saw a darkened silhouette run straight for the barn doors.

Ethan. It had to be. No one else would be so damned stupid and heroic all at once.

"No." She pounded on the window. No one heard her. She wanted to yell at them to stop him. "No!"

Wood creaked behind her.

Tansey whirled to face the door left open in

Ethan's haste to get outside and help his clan. Hope flashed that she'd been wrong, and he wasn't rushing headlong into danger. Maybe one of the others needed her. But neither Ethan nor one of his clan stood in the doorway.

Rye.

Tansey flung herself across the room and wrapped him in a tight hug. Then she took a step back and punched him hard in the chest.

"You asshole!" she yelled. Tears of relief and anger and frustration welled up at his sudden, shocking appearance. "Where have you been? Why did you leave? No note, nothing, just vanished into thin air? Didn't you know how worried I'd be?"

Her onslaught of questions stammered to a close. Rye didn't answer. He didn't react. His dead-eyed stare straight ahead chilled her to the bone and forced her to look beyond her initial excitement.

He wasn't the picture of health she remembered. Paler, lips drawn tight. His weight was off, maybe from living like a hermit for a few weeks. His greasy hair hadn't seen a brush in that time, she was sure.

"Rye?" she asked, softer than before.

"I'm sorry," he whispered. His eyes didn't move from the battle of fire outside the window.

Tansey broke out in a cold sweat. She looked

from her brother to the burning barn, then back to him again. Her hand raised to her gaping mouth of its own accord. Her entire body switched to autopilot as the realization smacked into her.

Rye set the fire.

"What did you do?" She stumbled several steps away from him.

A low whine squeezed out of him and he turned bright gold eyes on her. "Don't run from me."

Tansey raised her hands and tried to calm her racing heart. New shifters were dangerous. That'd been explained to her over and over since she arrived in Bearden. She didn't quite believe until that moment. Rye was her brother. He would never hurt her.

His wolf would, Ethan once said.

Rye lifted his nose and inhaled. "You smell afraid."

The action was one she'd seen from many shifters. None looked so animalistic as Rye. "There's a whole bunch of shifters outside fighting a fire that could spread with the wrong wind. Of course I'm afraid."

Maybe she could convince him it wasn't because of him. Maybe she could talk him down. She didn't appreciate feeling like the mouse caught between the cat's paws.

Or wolf's.

"I had to do it. All of it. Viho demanded it of me. Said this would clear my debts." The last word turned into another long whine.

"Debts?" She shook her head to tumble her thoughts into some semblance of order. "What debts? What are you talking about, Rye?"

She knew. She'd monitored his bank account. He had nothing but pennies to his name. Somehow, someway, they were connected to Viho. There were any number of ways to lose hard to an animal like that.

"You always were the tougher one. You got out. There was nothing to do after that. You left." Golden eyes focused on her again and his whine turned to a growl. "You left."

"Rye—Rye, you could have come with me any time. You know I'd always make room for you. We're brother and sister. That's what we do."

The swing in emotion left her off balance. Her Rye, not the strung-out copy in front of her, never voiced anything close to the accusation of abandonment.

Her Rye and the wolf were different.

Rye cocked his head at something Tansey couldn't hear. Then she caught it. Heavy footsteps slowly thumped across the wood floor of the house, like someone taking his time to peruse things that didn't belong to him. Each step felt like a nail driven into her coffin, death drawing nearer with every clunking step.

Out of the darkness, a lithe, dark-haired man materialized.

"Down, wolf," Viho ordered.

Rye immediately sank to his knees. His eyes bore holes in the floor.

All trace of power from Rye fled, right along with the air. Viho took up the entire room.

Tansey looked from one to the other as the puzzle pieces slid together. Pack business.

"How long, Rye?" she snapped. Her hands closed into fists. "How long have you planned this out?"

She left? No, that was on him. Hiding out and luring her from her life? Him, too. Where her brother ended and Viho's wolf began, she had no clue. Any departure point made her ill.

She worried her entire life about driving people away. She kept others at a distance to protect herself. There was no protection from the ones who abandoned her and still walked at her side. Betrayal cut deep wounds in her heart.

"Don't be mad at him, pretty flower. He only did what he was told. You weren't even a thought until I found you by pure accident." Viho grinned. "Then you were the perfect carrot to force my wayward wolf back into submission. And now you'll be the bait to bring down that fucking bear."

"All for what? So you can kill Ethan because of some fucked up family feud?" Good lord, he needed therapy. "Guess bad blood runs in the family."

"Killing him is too easy. Too clean. He needs to know loss. He needs everything he loves wiped out," Viho snarled.

"Don't hurt her," Rye whimpered. "Don't kill Tansey. That wasn't the deal."

Viho stroked a hand down Rye's head and raised his lips in a cold smile. "I'm not going to kill her," he reassured, dead eyes staring her down. "I'm going to turn her and ruin Ashford by claiming her for my own. Take her."

The last words whipped out of his mouth as an order and snapped Rye into action. Already bigger than her, the animal inside him only increased his strength.

"Rye, stop!" she pleaded. She didn't want to leave with him. She wanted nothing to do with Viho.

Tansey stumbled over her own feet trying to avoid her brother. Her slaps and punches didn't register. Even a kick landed on his shin did nothing to stop him.

She scrambled over the bed and met Viho waiting for her on the other side. She reached for anything to use as a weapon and wrapped her hands around a lamp on the nightstand. Viho laughed as the bulb cracked and shattered against the ground.

Rye handily snagged her arms from behind, clamped a hand over her mouth, and followed Viho out of the house and into the night.

CHAPTER 23

E than knew something was wrong the moment he stepped through his front door. All trace of exhaustion left him. The hair on the back of his neck stood on end.

His bear went silent.

The kitchen door swung in an uneasy breeze.

Strange scents filtered through his nose.

No, not strange enough. One belonged to Viho. The other had a tang of familiarity, but wasn't anyone he knew. They layered over each other, in and out along the same path.

Tansey.

Ethan darted straight for his bedroom. His jaw clenched as Viho's scent followed the exact same path.

Hope shriveled to nothing when he found the room empty.

His bear rampaged through his mind.

Their mate. Gone.

Sharp claws poked his palms when he clenched his fists. He should have come back to his woman, washed up and fallen back into bed with her to work off the agitation and exhaustion coursing through him. They had plans to make to get through the next days and weeks and months. They were going to feel each other out and see where they stood.

Instead, two unmated males entered his den and his mate was nowhere to be found.

"Fuck!" Ethan swung a fist into the wall. The flare of pain felt good. He wanted to feel that when he beat Viho into submission.

Because that meant he caught up to the asshole and set his mate free.

He could almost see what happened. Tansey's scent was still fresh. Fear and apprehension were strongest near the bed. But by the window, her anger had spiked. The scent he could recognize advanced to her there.

Fucking Viho. It wasn't enough to burn his barn with animals inside. He used it as a distraction to get to Tansey.

Ethan stalked out of the room, nostrils twitching with every deep inhale. In, then back out. Tansey's anger turned to fear the further through the living room they dragged her.

He found her phone tossed aside and broken near the fireplace.

He whirled at the sound of footsteps, a snarl raising his lips. The soot-covered faces of his clan watched him from just inside the front door.

"Viho took her. Find them," he snarled. They couldn't have gotten far. There still had to be a chance.

They didn't move fast enough.

Ethan grabbed the back of the nearest neck—Hunter—and dragged him through the great room and out the kitchen door.

"Find them," he snarled again.

His bear slammed into his chest and he did nothing to stop the beast. The sharp tips of claws lengthened from his fingernails. His clothes shredded as he dropped to the ground. Muscles broke apart and reformed new connections with the thicker, bigger bones of his inner animal. A full-bodied shake settled his fur.

Nothing settled the rage boiling in his veins.

The wolf stole onto his land and into his den. His livelihood was threatened.

His mate was taken.

He wanted blood.

Around him, the rest of the clan finished shifting. Eyes lowered as he swept a murderous gaze over them. The four pulses of life inside his head tried to shrink back as much as the bears in front of him.

War had arrived.

Ethan roared his challenge into the night.

ETHAN DRUMMED his fingers on the bar at Defiant Dog and waited impatiently for his drink to arrive. He downed the shot as soon as it was slid to him and slammed the glass back down.

"Another," he growled.

By the Broken, he needed the liquor. The warmth spread through him and made him feel a flash of... something. That flicker of emotion, be it rage over the injustice or grief of a denied future, was better than the ice that chilled him from the moment he lost Tansey's scent at the edge of his land.

Was that how it started with his father? Needing to feel anything at all?

Ethan frowned at the whiskey sloshing in the shot glass, then gulped it down.

"Another."

What did all those crime shows Colette loved to watch say? Missing people were rarely found after two days. The outliers were so small that he was better off hoping for some device to travel time and spirit her away before the point of abduction than thinking she'd ever be back in his arms.

Day one ticked to a close without a damn sign of her anywhere.

There was no losing his shit. He'd lost it within the first hour.

Everything hurt. His bear wouldn't stop roaring in his head. He had no leads. He wanted to drown out the pain that made him feel like he'd taken a bath in acid.

His mate was stolen from him and he couldn't find her. Failure was not an option, and yet she still remained apart from him.

"Another."

That they took her alive was something. It was all he had left to cling to. Viho took Tansey alive to use as some fucked up piece of his game. Ethan just needed to wait and see how it played out.

Too bad he was never good at waiting.

Defiant Dog was his last hope of finding something to go on. Viho wouldn't make the mistake of showing his face inside Bearden, but maybe one of his stupider pack mates would stray into the dive bar at the edge of the enclave.

And if not, he intended to get well and truly sloshed.

He'd snapped at every person he'd come across so much that his clan avoided meeting his eyes or sticking near him for longer than it took to receive a new order. He'd reduced all four men to shaking messes whenever they were forced to interact. They didn't deserve it, and he couldn't help it. His bear was out of control and grabbed hold of power wherever it could be found.

They'd searched all night with him and zipped through emergency work when the light of dawn colored the sky. Fences were checked, the herd and horses secured and treated for any burns, then they were right back to prowling the territory.

Every last one of them came up empty.

He'd lost count of how many times he followed the faint trace of wolf scent from his den to the kitchen door and then off the property where she'd been shoved into a vehicle. Dozens, at least.

He still had no sign of Tansey.

The bar door swung open and Ethan dipped the brim of his hat. The scent of fur, gas, and grease clung to the newcomer. Wolf. He didn't wear the vest that marked him part of the Vagabonds nor did he carry a hint of Viho in his scent, but he wasn't anyone from the enclave.

Jesse and Alex trailed in after the wolf. Neither looked at him, but they took up spots near the door. Once settled, Jesse passed a bland look over the room and nodded once.

Ethan raised his fingers and ordered a beer while the wolf leaned against the other end of the bar. He followed up on the signal by faking a trip to the outhouse. His beer waited for him when he returned.

He grabbed the bottle by the neck and slid unsteadily down the bar to the wolf. Anger burned through the shots he'd down. Viho dared send someone to watch him? Maybe he wouldn't need to wait long before the hunt resumed.

Ethan tightened the leash on his bear and added a stumble to his performance for good measure. "Hey, that your ride out front? Pretty sweet Harley if it is."

The wolf grunted. "She's mine."

"Must really hurt when she gets a scratch, huh?"

The man rose up from his barstool with a pissed

off glare. Alex and Jesse jumped up from their spots and crowded against his back before he could get far.

Ethan crossed his arms over his chest and pointed to the barstool. "You work for the Vagabonds?" Subtle went out the window after the third hour without his mate.

He waved a dismissive hand. "Once or twice. I'm not going to turn away money."

"You know where they're holed up?" The motel where he'd grabbed Tansey's things the first night she blew into his life was another dead end. The nearby bars hadn't seen Viho or a Vagabond in days.

"No."

Ethan took a swig of his beer. "Lie."

The wolf growled and slammed the bottom of his bottle against the bar. He swung jagged edges at Ethan, only catching his shirt as he jumped back.

He threw himself to the side and shoved the shifter off balance. A savage twist of his wrist dropped the broken bottle. Good. He wanted it to be a fair match.

He wasn't about to let old Hector ruin his fight again. He seized the wolf by the scruff of his neck and threw him out the door.

Ethan followed right on his heels. He grabbed a

handful of the man's shirt and threw a punch into his face. Blood spurted from his busted nose, but Ethan wasn't done. He shoved the wolf shifter into his own motorcycle, sending man and machine tumbling to the ground.

Almost too quick to track, the shifter jumped to his feet and dove for Ethan. His arms locked around his waist and sent him falling hard on his back. His bear roared in his head to rip and tear and slice.

Yes.

No.

Tansey. They needed information. A dead man would give them nothing.

He threw a punch into the man's middle and whipped them back over. "Where the fuck are they?" he snarled.

The wolf grinned, blood coloring his teeth. "They're going to destroy you."

Ethan roared and pounded the man with his fists. It felt good to let out the bloodlust that'd plagued his bear for the last twenty-four hours. While it wasn't Viho, the wolf was a good stand-in until he could fight the real thing.

"Where?" he demanded again.

The wolf laughed, so he hit him again. And again.

Fucking assholes needed to learn some manners

and he would be the fucker to teach them. Taking a woman unconnected to their old fight? Taking her brother and wrecking her family? Using her to bait him?

Tansey needed help. He needed her back. He didn't care how many wolves he had to tear apart to find her.

"Ethan." Jesse grabbed his fist before he could land another blow. "Let him go."

"Fuck that," he snarled at his second. The scent of blood was in the air and he wanted to feel bone crunch under his fists.

"We have to get back to Black Claw. Hunter spotted something."

The pure, unadulterated rage pumping through him with each beat of his heart fell from a violent boil to a simmer. He let go of the wolf and stood, leaving him with one last sharp kick to the ribs. Whatever Hunter found was more important than one small-time asshole. "Let's go."

CHAPTER 24

Tansey didn't know where Rye and Viho and the rest of the scum-sucking Vagabonds took her. Once it became apparent that she wasn't going to head into captivity willingly and cease all her kicking and struggling like a good little kidnap victim, Viho slammed his fist into the back of her head and poof—out went the lights.

Everything hurt when she woke up the first time.

Fire burned outward from her throbbing forearm. Blood flecked off from where it'd welled and dried during her unconsciousness. A ring of jagged cuts didn't look as bad as she thought they should for all the pain that laced through her.

The room swam. Blackness danced at the edges

of her vision, then swooped over her with no care for what she wanted.

Everything still hurt the second time darkness parted for a noisy, smelly reality. She thought she turned to her side and heaved out the entire contents of her stomach.

The third time, that seemed to be the charm. Everything still hurt and her mouth tasted like she'd eaten the contents of a dumpster, but she no longer felt the overwhelming urge to give up the ghost.

Weak, Tansey lifted her head and tried to get her bearings. The room was hardly bigger than a closet, with only one door. Her head ached anytime someone spoke or laughed on the other side. She lay on a thin mattress left on the middle of the floor.

Her arm throbbed in time with her heart. She couldn't put any weight on it. Until she rolled her head to the side, she thought it'd been taken clean off.

Dried blood covered her arm. The marks she thought she saw earlier were almost hidden by the swelling.

Tansey carefully pressed her fingertips to the angry flesh. Pain flared to life and left her gasping. Her stomach clenched hard enough to curve her in on herself.

A high-pitched whine blew from her lips. That wasn't normal. She needed help.

The piercing sound of metal scraping against itself made Tansey wince. Smoke and fur and booze and unwashed bodies slammed into her as the door swung open.

Rye slunk inside, eyes never lifting from the ground. He bumped the door closed behind him and shuffled to her mattress, then sank to his knees next to her.

Something... soft brushed against her mind. She wanted to bare her teeth at her brother.

"It's going to be okay," Rye told her. "You're almost out of the worst part. I made it through. We have the same genes. You'll make it, I know."

Tansey struggled to sit up. Her limbs didn't want to move except in the most uncoordinated and jerky way. She felt like she'd downed half her body weight of pure alcohol and then gotten into a fight with a tank.

Rye's scent invaded her nose. She could practically taste the grease in his hair. Too many onions on his last meal, too. He'd always had a fondness for them.

But more than that, she wanted to bite him. He'd hurt her. Betrayed her. Let her think something terrible had happened to him while she uprooted her entire life. And for what? So his new BFF could play head games with Ethan?

That softness rubbed against her again and her stomach sank with longing. Even more than the desire to get away from wherever she was being held, she felt the need to get back to Ethan. She wanted his earthy scent in her nose and his arms caging her in protection.

Ethan wasn't there. Rye was. Viho. Other Vagabonds. They deserved to be put in their places.

A growl rattled in her throat.

Wait.

A growl?

Scared she knew the answer, she asked, "What did you do to me?"

Rye cupped her cheeks to hold her head steady. She tried to push his hands away, but he had the strength of a grown man and a shifter while she felt about as strong as a day old kitten.

"What, Rye?" She needed to hear the words.

"Shush," Rye chided. "You'll be fine. This is what you wanted, isn't it? To help me? Soon you'll do that on four feet instead of just two."

Four feet. Motherfucking Viho actually bit her. And Rye let it happen. Her skin crawled to be anywhere near him. He'd helped someone steal a big choice from her and talked like it was no big deal.

"This isn't how I hoped helping you would go." She twisted out of his grasp and grimaced when her nose picked up a new scent.

Nope. She hadn't made it fully over the side of the dank mattress. Gross.

Almost as gross as wondering what other messes had been made on the bed.

"Where are we?" she whispered. Anything else sounded too loud.

She needed an idea of where they were and what direction to head when she finally made it to her feet. No way would she stick around for whatever insanity Viho had planned next.

"A place Viho keeps up. He has interests in the area. Don't worry about that now. You're doing so good."

"I don't care about that!" she snapped.

That new, inner instinct of hers whined out of frustration. Too weak. Still too weak for anything.

Tansey squeezed her eyes shut and focused on herself. Her own thoughts. People thoughts. Unless she was going to sprout fur and fangs, she didn't want anything else intruding.

Not good enough. More of that other side

pressed against her. It tried to devour her. Needles slid into her brain, under her skin. Darkness closed around her and tried to beat her down into nothing. She felt like her mind was being ripped in half.

"Why?" Tansey growled. She wasn't even sure which entity to direct the question. Her other half, her brother, any of the assholes in the outer room, they could all go to hell.

Rye rocked back on his heels. His voice edged into the same whine he used when he spoke to Viho. "I need this, Tansey. Viho… He has plans and you're a part of them now. I tried to keep you out of it, but you just couldn't mind your own business, could you?"

"No. You're not blaming me for caring." She cracked open one eye. "You're my brother; that's what I'm supposed to do. You didn't have to do any of this. Rye, you still don't. Get us out of here. Please."

"I can't do that. I can't disobey him," Rye whispered. He shoved his hair out of his eyes and had the decency to look pained. "You don't say no to a man like Viho. When you don't have anything else to offer him, he'll take your loyalty. He turned me, Tans. He let me get a taste of his blood, gamble everything away to afford that next hit, and turned me into one of them when I lost it all. Said he had plans for me to pay him back."

"What plans, Rye?" He shook his head, so she pressed again. "What plans?"

Addict, in more ways than one. That was what Rye kept hidden from her. He let Viho put poison in her to pay off his debts. She'd worked her ass off to find her own path and then to afford to locate him. Yet when his world spiraled out of control, he took the easy way out and ran.

The betrayal hurt almost as much as realizing he was just like their dad. Only instead of just disappearing, he had to drag her down with him.

She must have said the last out loud, because Rye shook his head.

"You shouldn't have looked for me," he insisted. "You should have left well enough alone. I ran to keep you safe. I didn't want Viho snaring you into anything. You were a weakness. A liability. I tried to protect you."

"Fuck you, Rye." She lifted her chin and tried to meet his gaze, but he kept ducking her eyes. That pissed her off even more. "You want me to cry for you? After you let him turn me, too? Own your shit."

She had all the sympathy in the world for him, but none of that changed the choices he made or the consequences he brought down on her head. He didn't want to drag her into his mess? He should have picked up the damn phone and told her that.

The door banged open and Viho stood in the middle, hands on his hips and a wild grin lifting his lips. "She awakens!"

Gruff laughter rose from the Vagabonds in the outer room.

Viho crouched next to her. "How is our pretty flower?"

Tansey recoiled when his hands took hold of her much the same as Rye. Viho thumbed open one eyelid, then the other. She jerked her head out of his grasp before he could do anything else.

"Good. Won't be long now. We got eyes on your boyfriend. Wouldn't want to keep him waiting."

"Fuck you," she ground out.

Viho clicked his tongue. "Mind your language when speaking to your alpha. Wouldn't want to wash that mouth out with soap."

"Fuck you," she hissed. "You're nothing to me. I won't have any part in your plans."

Something forceful slammed into her chest. She wanted to bite him. Rip him into pieces. Make him cower beneath her fangs.

For a single second, she thought she saw worry

in Viho's eyes. Then the concern packed itself away, and he was all slimy confidence again.

"What are you going to do, pretty flower? Can you even stand on your feet yet?" Viho favored her with an infuriating smirk then looked over his shoulder and whistled. All noise in the outer room snapped to silence. "Pack it in, boys. We're going on a bear hunt!"

Howls rose and fell into another round of laughter.

"No. Leave them alone." She wanted to force him to her will, make him give up his stupid quest. Years had passed and lives were settled since the original feud between fathers. It was time to move away from the past.

Viho whipped his attention back to her with a growl. "I told you before. I'm going to strip everything away from that man just like his father did to me. I already turned his mate. I want him to see you submit to another before the life dies in his eyes."

Mate. The word felt... heavy in one part of her mind. The other recognized it, logically, as something between shifters.

The logical side wasn't the one itching to taste Viho's blood for threatening Ethan.

"You didn't know, did you? Humans," he scoffed.

He cocked his head with cruelty in his eyes. "Or maybe he didn't tell you. Poor, poor little flower. Your brother disappears without a word and your mate doesn't even want you. You could say I'm doing you a favor. I reunited you with one and will save you the pain of another."

"You're a dickhead and I hope you get your ass kicked tonight."

"You'll be there to watch it, sugar." He rose to his feet and walked backward into the outer room. "Bring her," he ordered.

CHAPTER 25

Ethan stood in the center of his territory with his arms crossed and waited. For what, he wasn't sure. Hunter spotted a single motorcycle scouting the road, then nothing else. The wolf at Defiant Dog was another clue.

Electricity crackled in the air as if lightning struck the ground next to him. A storm was coming, and soon.

The others spread out at his sides. Alex cracked his neck and shook out his arms. Hunter and Lorne grimaced into the darkness. Jesse folded his arms over his chest and waited with a blank look on his face.

In his head, the tiny studs that connected him to each of them tensed. He needed to finish this once and for all. Viho had pressed and goaded until this was the only conclusion. He needed to keep his clan alive. War had come for them and it was his job as alpha to usher them to the other side.

A rumble in the distance drew his attention. The noise of it built, louder and lower, strumming through his body like a deep bass.

No headlights lit the road, but the unmistakable sound of tires clanking over cattle grates told when the Valdana pack crossed over to his land.

Engines revved and roared as they neared. Most didn't slow, following the lead in a wide circle around his clan. Ethan didn't need more than a passing glance to know who rode at the head.

On the second pass, Viho tossed a body off his lap.

Blood tinged the air as the person bounced and rolled to a stop mere feet from his boots. Ethan's heart faltered to a stop.

Tansey.

Not just her, either. There was something more to her scent under all the blood and sweat and sick. Something like moonlight and deep woods, and growing stronger by the second.

"You turned her," he said flatly, following Viho on another round.

The clan at his side tensed. Boots scuffed in the dirt and fists clenched at their sides.

Fuck. *Fuck!* His bear sounded off in his head with the same sentiment. Fucking Viho turned Tansey, no doubt against her will. The crime alone meant death for a shifter even without the heavy-handed laws humans tried to place on them.

It wasn't only the perverse act that hollowed his middle and pounded blood in his veins. She'd be a wolf. The intimacy of turning her himself—if she chose—was stolen.

Survival wasn't guaranteed, either. Women handled it better than men, but even that wasn't a sure bet. The uncontrolled shaking of the woman before him didn't bode well for her transition.

His. Mate.

His bear ripped him to shreds for the delay in taking Viho apart piece by piece.

He and Tansey had been thrust together and set up to be enemies from the start. Instead, they were drawn together like a pair of magnets. No matter the distance or obstacles between them, they were pulled back to one another.

Did he know the future? No. But he knew she was in it and he'd fall to his knees if something happened to rip her from it. They needed to make everything up to one another. He needed to do more than just provide. He needed to put himself on the line and stay there. There was no backing up when shit got tough for a woman like Tansey. He needed to have her back through it all.

She was the distraction he needed. The balance in his world. She'd keep him from tripping too far and winding up full circle in the place his father had ended. There was more to life than proving himself against a ghost.

He glanced to one side, then the other. The men who stood with him and the woman on the ground at his feet were what truly mattered. He'd be the best damn person he could for his clan and family.

At that moment, doing so required blood to spill.

Viho hit the kickstand with his heel and settled his motorcycle into place. The others circled in a slower path than before, widening the path to cage in their leader.

"Last chance, Ashford. Walk away with your life or see everything you hold dear burned to ashes just like your father did to my mother."

"He honored her more than your father ever did," Ethan spat. "He could have left her to rot. She got the same sending off as mine."

Three sets of eyes shined in the night to his left. Four blinked at his right.

"They're everywhere," Jesse muttered from his side.

Distraction. The wolves on bikes clogged the air with roaring engines and the scent of exhaust to hide the streaming force surrounding them from all sides. How many answered to Viho, Ethan didn't know. Viho's pack, maybe others allied with him for reasons of their own, he didn't care. They'd all be dead by morning if he had his way.

They shouldn't have threatened his mate and his clan.

The last of the engines died and Viho's enforcers joined him in snarling their victory. Too many eyes watched from the darkness with too many growls.

The air tensed, then exploded into action.

A huge, black wolf charged Alex before he had the chance to shift. Fangs latched on to his arm as he and the wolf slammed into the ground.

Next to him, a blond bear ripped out of Hunter. On Ethan's other side, Jesse and Lorne let their inner animals take their skin with roars loud enough to hurt his ears.

They held their own. The battle for him was with Viho.

But... Tansey.

"Ethan."

His whispered name was accompanied by a shaking hand inching toward him. Fuck Viho. He couldn't leave her in the middle of a fight. Too many mouths sought out flesh. He wouldn't have her further harmed.

"Kill him." Gold light flared in her eyes at the order.

His bear sawed through his control in desperation to get free.

Wolves dove for him. Jaws snapped and caught arms he raised to protect his face and neck.

He let his bear burst from his skin.

Ethan latched onto one wolf's neck and shook the creature savagely until it hung limp from his jaws. The one on his back was just an annoyance, something to be forgotten in his drive to protect Tansey. He rose up on his hind legs and shook the wolf from his form, then slammed back down to all fours and bit hard on the wolf's back foot with a sickening crunch.

Three more tried to pull him away from Tansey. He blasted huge paws into one and sent him flying through the air. The other two bit and slashed at his sides, leaving long gashes he refused to feel. They, too, joined the ones that didn't move.

Too many. Far too many. Each one put down was replaced with another. Still more watched from the sidelines.

Jesse lumbered up to his side. Hunter took up his other side. Blood matted their fur.

Alex and Lorne tore into any wolf that came near, both digging deep into the anger they carried. Alex wore his with pride while Lorne buried his deep, but the rage served them both in a battle for their lives.

A battle they were losing.

Viho padded forward with murder in his eyes. He paced back and forth, tail lowered and ears flat against his head. His snarl was the loudest thing in the world.

Ethan wanted blood. Jesse and Hunter dug in their feet and gave him tiny glances.

Clan. Their bonds ran deeper than blood. They chose one another. They had each other's backs. If he needed to fight, they would watch his mate.

Ethan stepped over Tansey and toward Viho. Win or lose the war, he was determined to come out against one final battle.

The roar of a lion jerked his attention from the circling wolf for a split second. There, near the burnt wreckage of his barn, Trent stood with his pride. Ethan doubted he'd ever been so glad to see the prickly man.

He roared his greeting to the reinforcements and watched the lions run straight for the fight.

TAWNY PAWS and black manes streaked past her. The meeting of flesh shook the ground even before the whines and yelps of pain registered in her head.

Tansey wobbled as she inched her way toward the front door of Ethan's home. She needed protection. Safety. Neither of which were in the middle of a war. And Ethan needed to fight without hovering over her. She hindered his ability to battle for his life, land, and clan.

He fought for her. She drove him away early on, but they kept circling back to one another. In the thick of it, he stayed over her and kept her safe. Those were the actions of a man who would stick around when she needed him the most.

She wouldn't let Viho goad her into bad thoughts of abandonment and betrayal.

The fire coursing through her veins stretched

painful fingers through her brain. She'd never needed anyone more than that moment. She wanted to find her feet and a gun and help take care of business. All she could manage was an inch forward at a time.

Dammit, she'd make it out alive. She'd barricade herself behind doors and let Ethan sort the rest out.

Fangs sank into her leg and ripped her screaming backward.

Pain. Pain. So much pain. Wetness covered her leg where the wolf latched on. Her weak kicks were nothing to the big beast.

Before her eyes, the wolf shimmered and a big man crouched over her. Viho snarled, her blood still coating his teeth.

Viho grabbed her by the throat and hauled her to her feet. She wheezed and clawed at the fingers holding her upright. Too tight. Too terrible.

"Ashford!" Viho yelled.

The fight still raged on around them. Lions joined with bears in tearing into any wolf they could snag with claw or fang. The stench of blood turned her stomach.

But they three existed in a bubble all on their own.

Bones snapped and his shape shimmered. Tansey

blinked back the darkness and found Ethan rising to his feet.

"Let her go, asshole," Ethan snapped.

Rage soaked him from head to toe. Silver eyes churned with it. His shoulders were tight and his chest bloody. Even his strong jaw clenched hard enough to break teeth.

Glorious. There was no other word for it. He was like some Greek god intent on waging war until the last soul on the battlefield was his to claim.

She wanted to stand at his side.

Viho shook her slightly and brought her back to painful reality where her limbs didn't want to work and her thoughts edged into insanity.

"You want this one?" he growled. "She's already been turned."

The sense of other in her middle rolled through her with disgust. She didn't belong to anyone. Certainly not the man using her for revenge.

"Let her go."

"She's pack, now. There's no letting her go. Strong, too, if a little mouthy. The brother doesn't have half her will. I'll beat it out of her, don't worry."

Searing pain washed through Tansey. Spots gathered at the edges of her vision and closed in with debilitating quickness.

Coward, she wanted to call him. He wouldn't meet Ethan in a fair fight. He had to prick open a wound and dig deep into it. There was nothing honorable about his revenge.

She chanted the word over and over in her head. *Coward. Coward.*

The only sounds that left her were baby snarls.

Ethan's eyes flicked from her face to Viho's. She pleaded with him to end it.

Viho dragged his nose to the crook of her neck. "Maybe I'll keep her for my own."

"No!"

Another wolf sprang forward. He didn't go for any lion or bear. He went straight for Viho.

Tansey fell from Viho's hold as the man twisted to meet the challenge.

Rye.

The red wolf snapped his jaws in Viho's face. Viho slammed his fist into the wolf's head. In the brief second where the stunned wolf shook his head, Viho slipped from one form to the other.

Viho's lips raised in a snarl. His head lowered to the ground and his tail stiffened between his legs. Hot anger boiled off him.

From the corner of her eye, Tansey spotted a huge lion creeping closer. Murder shined in his eyes, and she knew it wouldn't matter who got in his way.

She scrambled out of the lion's path just as he clipped Viho's hind legs.

She fell back into the dirt and watched a bear's belly fly overhead. Four paws landed in the dirt on her other side.

Ethan hit Viho again when he whirled to attack the lion. Rye darted in and nipped him, then darted right back out before Viho could spin back around.

Outside the circle, lions and bears still tore into the massive wolves that attacked. Blood wet the earth beneath their paws.

Then something changed.

The lion raked a gruesome path down Viho's side just as Ethan closed his jaws around the wolf's tail. Viho yelped and jumped away from them both. Free for a moment, he lifted his snout and let loose a long, mournful howl.

Then ran.

The other wolves reacted almost as one. Some shifted and made their way to their motorcycles. Others faded into the darkness. Most turned tail and followed after Viho.

Cowards. Cowards, all of them. Tansey tried to yell the word after them, and only managed a growl.

Then Ethan was there, picking her up and dragging her into his lap. Her whole body shook with adrenaline dumping into her veins and the fire Viho put there, too. Another growl rattled in her throat, but it wasn't her. Not her.

That *other* one.

Pain, so much pain. It split her head worse than any headache she'd ever experienced.

Blood and sweat clogged Ethan's scent. He stroked her hair from her face and dragged his gaze up and down her form. "Tansey, Tansey," he murmured. "Strong woman. Strong wolf. She's is trying to buck his control even before she's born."

"Stop it," she mouthed. Darkness crept further through her, narrowing her eyesight down to pinpricks. Her heart stuttered.

Sadness took his silver eyes straight to a mournful blue. "I don't... I don't know how."

Somewhere nearby, someone clicked his tongue in disgust. Trent, she thought.

"Bite her. Can't you see she's going mad? She needs to know where she belongs."

"That's not my call to make," Ethan snapped.

"Then say your goodbyes, because that wolf is ripping her apart. Ground her to you if you want a chance to save her."

"Fuck."

Silver flashed above her. His eyes, she thought.

"Tansey," he whispered in her ear. "This isn't how I wanted to do this. You can hate me later if you want, but know I'll still be happy because you'll be alive."

She tried to nod.

That other side scrabbled to get free of the weak, dying body caging her in.

Then there was pain. So much pain. Over the same bite Viho placed on her skin, Ethan sank his teeth into her flesh.

Tansey gasped, body nearly jerking out of his lap. Her heart thundered in her chest, pounding harder than if she'd run a thousand miles without stopping. Her lungs struggled to keep up.

The wolf settled down into watchful silence. The bear was powerful. Worthy.

Theirs.

Instincts she didn't understand slammed into her and blazed the word across her mind. She'd always wanted something special that couldn't be torn away from her, and Ethan had just given her that.

Tansey breathed an easy sigh and let her eyes close.

CHAPTER 26

"What are you doing out of bed?"

Tansey jerked straight, then glowered in Ethan's direction. Not even the sight of him fresh out of a shower after a day spent building a new barn could calm her jitters. She felt caged up and useless.

He'd waited on her hand and foot since the night of Viho's attack, and forbade her from leaving bed. If she wanted something, she needed to call him. Water? He kept the glass by her side of the bed full. Breakfast, lunch, and dinner? Served on a tray only after he propped a wall of pillows behind her back.

She enjoyed the treatment for the first twelve hours, but after being chided for stepping across the room for her phone charger, she'd had enough.

"I'm getting something to drink. I can manage that."

He stared at her flatly. "You should still be in bed. Until your wolf—"

"I know. But it's been five days of absolute boredom and still no sign of this furry mess."

She'd stabilized right out in the middle of a war zone. Her breath evened out and the spots in her eyes faded. She even recognized the ticklish feeling in her brain and the rumbles in her middle were from a separate entity from her original self.

That was as close as Tansey Prime and Tansey Wolf came to an understanding. She—the human half—waited for anything further from her inner wolf. That furry broad was happy to stay locked away indefinitely.

Unfortunate, that. Worry creased not just Ethan's face, but the entire clan the longer her wolf didn't show herself. Three days, max, from the time of a bite to the first shift and she edged closer to double that with each minute that ticked by.

What could she say? She made everything difficult.

The days of staring at the ceiling and sneaking out of bed while Ethan left to tend the ranch were filled with constant wondering of what would have happened had she never accepted Viho's offer to track her brother. Both Rye and Viho were still thorns in her side.

Viho was still out there, somewhere. Ethan's clan and Trent's pride chased down the ones they could, but neither turned up the mastermind behind the attack. By the time Chief Hawkins pulled up with flashing lights and cruisers behind him, there were no living wolves to be found. The man left empty-handed and with curses on his lips about war being bad for the enclave.

Well, sure. Tell that to the asshole who started it.

Rye, too, was gone. He at least had the decency to call her before disappearing into the wind again. Ethan glared at the phone the entire conversation, which truthfully hadn't been long.

She'd given him terse answers when he asked if she was okay. A rift had grown between them, and she wasn't sure if she could ever forgive him for his role in turning her life upside down. At least he was free of Viho and wanted to make his own way in the world.

At least he could get a damn glass of water whenever he pleased.

Ethan took a step toward her and his scent flipped a switch inside her. Her frustrated inner rantings were replaced by a tongue stuck to the roof of her mouth and a heart pounding against her breastbone.

Muscles rippled under his skin with his slow advance. Her fingers curled into her palm to keep from rushing right to him and licking a path down his stomach.

Hello, cowboy.

Ethan paused before his next step and swept his gaze up and down her body. His nostrils flared, catching her scent, too. His lips twitched with a smile he tried to keep contained.

Too bad she could smell his amused smugness.

And his lust. The towel wrapped around his waist did little to hide the tent pole growing underneath.

Sexy, sexy man. She didn't know what she'd done to deserve a man like him.

Her wolf sat up in a hurry. Ethan always pulled her beast to the forefront of her mind. The saucy little wolf wanted to rub up and down his big body.

The images—sendings, Ethan called them— weren't the only reactions the wolf spawned around Ethan. Tansey wanted to sink her teeth in him almost constantly.

Another experience denied, much to her frustration.

"I'm fine," she said a little breathlessly. "Better than fine."

He wrapped his arms around her waist and lifted her easily. His eyes stayed on her as he carried her from the kitchen and back into the bedroom, where he sat on the edge of the bed. Tansey dragged her lips down his jaw.

"You need to rest," he said in a choked voice.

Victory. "I need to help get this place running. I can't do that when you keep me confined to bed without all the fun parts."

"You still want that?" Him, too, he left unsaid.

"I thought I made myself clear in wanting to see where this would go."

"I know, but—" He cut himself off with a curse, then lifted her arm. The marks didn't line up. One was much more savage and held a silvery sheen in the right light. That came from Viho.

The smaller one was more in line with a human mouth, but no less jagged from his bear's fangs. Brushing his fingers over it spread fire through her veins.

"Neither of these were your choice," he said solemnly.

"They're my choice now." She pressed her lips to his, then drew back so he could see the truth in her eyes. "I get to decide what I do from now on, and I'm picking you."

She slid to the floor between his legs before he could object. Her fingers untucked the edge of his towel. Ethan reached for the hem of her shirt and tugged it over her head.

"Do I bite you?" The wolf in her mind whined and bounced on her feet. That sounded like a damn good idea.

"It only seems fair." He wrapped a hand around her wrist and held her steady. Seriousness tightened his jaw. "Tansey, don't do this unless you want it."

Want. She wanted him. Human side, stubborn wolf, both were in agreement.

Ethan already claimed her. She wanted to do the same. It was a white lie when she said she wanted to consider their future. Deep down, she already knew it belonged with him. The wolf said as much and Tansey felt the absolute rightness in that instinct.

She bit her bottom lip and smiled innocently up at him, crawling her fingers up his thighs. "Are you going to fight me?"

Ethan's eyes rolled back in his head and he let off a rough breath. "Only if you keep talking."

"No dirty talk?" she purred. The sigh of ecstasy when she wrapped her hand around his shaft spread warmth through her belly. "No telling you how much I want to taste you?"

"Bad wolf."

She pumped his length once. Still holding his eyes with hers, she dragged her tongue from the base to the tip and slid her mouth over him.

"Very bad wolf," he groaned.

His fingers twisted into her hair and cupped the base of her skull. His grip stayed light, more like he needed to feel her rather than guiding her movement or forcing her down.

Touch. Her wolf demanded it, too.

Tansey sucked on him, sliding up and down his cock. His breath hitched each time she rose up again and his fingers tightened in her hair on every beat down. Low growls and groans bubbled out of him. She loved hearing him, loved knowing she caused those noises to trickle out of him.

Heat whipped through her. She needed more.

She rose up on her knees without changing her pace and slid her hand between her legs. Her head swam with the need coursing through her veins. Him. He was all she wanted and holy hot damn, her body was ready for him. She couldn't resist rocking against her hand for the tiny bit of relief it afforded her.

Ethan's eyes churned silver when she flicked a glance upward. "Take those off. Let me see," he said in a gravelly voice.

Tansey wiggled out of her panties and resumed her place between his thighs. She spread her legs wider, rolling her eyes upward and meeting his smoldering look. She slid her mouth up and down his shaft and matched it with touching herself. His breath quickened with more licks, more strokes, until his control slipped. He lifted his hips each time she drew him in, sliding deeper with each thrust.

"Fuck... Tansey," Ethan gritted out. "Come here."

She didn't need to be told twice, but couldn't help herself teasing him more. Slow, so slow, she licked him again before crawling onto his lap.

A lazy smile graced his lips. He dropped back onto one elbow, then another, hot and raw gaze sweeping over her body and lingering on her curves. "You taking charge, bad wolf?"

She followed him down, planting her hands on his chest and leaning forward to lick his lips. She jerked back when he tried to chase her into a deeper kiss. "Maybe I am. I got turned by an alpha wolf and mated by an alpha bear. What more did you expect?"

"Mouthiness. Not listening to sense. More of the same, really." His lips twitched into a crooked smirk.

She rocked herself against his cock and relished watching his grin disappear into a pleasured groan. So thick. So hard. Her mouth fell open as she eased down an inch, then up, teasing him.

A growl rattled in her chest and she slapped her hands over her mouth in surprise. That was going to take some getting used to.

Ethan pried her hands away and sipped at her lips. "Don't hide her away." He kissed her again. "She's part of you now."

Tansey moved over him again. Easy. Steady. He filled her completely, and then some. And with the burst of pleasure came another rough noise in her throat.

With a growl, he surged into her, hips thrusting up to meet hers. The first stroke, and pressure already squeezed her down. Another, and she was ready to spring.

Play, that was what he allowed her. He let her have her fun, but he was the one in charge. She couldn't get enough of it.

A growl rumbled in his throat and he gripped the back of her neck. He pushed off the bed and met her halfway, wrapping his other arm around her to hold her tight. His lips crashed against hers, devouring her, as he moved them into a perfect rhythm.

She couldn't keep steady. He overwhelmed all her senses and called to the wolf inside her. His earthy scent was made to drown in. His hands, rough from hard work, dragged fire across her skin. Deep grunts mingled with her softer cries until she lost the beat.

Ethan surged into action, rolling them over and taking control. She buried her face in the crook of his neck, tasting the salt on his skin.

He gripped her hip and bucked hard into her, driving the pressure through the roof. So close. Him, too, if the sense of urgency was what she thought.

She needed more.

That other part of her had been born in fear and anguish. Ethan wrapped her in something else entirely. At her lowest moment, when she didn't know how to manage the extra senses and thoughts running through her mind and trying to take control, he'd tied a string around her heart and dragged her back to earth. He tethered her in her moment of desperation.

More. *More.*

The instinct was strong enough to rattle a tiny growl in her throat.

He gripped the back of her head and held her close. "Do it," he dared. "Bite me. Mark me."

Yes. Yes, that was right. That was what she needed.

She needed to bring them closer together and finish what he started.

Tansey kissed down Ethan's jaw and throat. A sexy snarl vibrated his chest and skittered goose bumps over her arms. Inside her, his cock twitched.

"Do it," he growled.

Good, so good. Almost too good. He thrust into her harder, faster, dragging against all her nerves. Electricity built between them, higher and higher, until she could hardly breathe.

More.

Tansey licked a long line down his neck and dragged her lips across his shoulder. Then she pressed her teeth against his skin and bit.

Ethan roared, not with any hint of pain. Ecstasy, pure bliss, that was in the sexiest growl she'd ever heard. There were no words to describe it, nothing he could say, other than that groan of pleasure.

A sting of pain on her own shoulder sent her careening over the edge. Warmth flooded her with his release as he pulsed deep inside.

He held her close, fingers tight in her hair, and slowly moved with her until the last of their aftershocks faded.

He eased her away to look in her eyes. "That's how it should have been done," he said against her mouth, his voice tight with emotion. "Not forced or backed into a corner. Because we wanted it."

She wanted him. Forever.

Her choice. Her heart. She wanted to live in a world where she had a place at Ethan's side. She wanted to argue until they turned blue and make up for it until the sun rose the next day. Tough days were ahead of them, but he'd given her exactly what she needed: himself.

EPILOGUE

Tansey growled. She was supposed to be a graceful, elegant creature. Sleek, swift, silent. A deadly hunter on four legs.

Instead, she walked like a dog with booties placed on its paws. Her limbs didn't work. They were too long, too many, and she had no control.

Ethan laughed.

She snarled. Or tried to. A whine was all that came out.

How could a man smell that good? Her animal side wanted to yip and yap and bounce around like one of those ankle biter dogs. Except every time she tried, she tumbled from one side to the other. Drunken sailors could walk a straighter line.

"Stop treating them like they're stilts. Those are your legs; make them work," he said between breaths, wiping tears from his eyes.

Tears!

Tansey crouched down and bunched those limbs he said would so easily obey underneath her, then sprang for him.

She fell flat on her face and Ethan laughed harder.

She took several more minutes before she gained some control over her new limbs. The tail really gave her trouble. It helped her balance, but also kept spooking her. The black tip flashing just over her shoulder looked like something zooming right for her.

Ethan laughed at the sudden starts and panicked twists, too.

He stopped laughing when she finally packed her legs underneath her and jumped into him hard enough to knock him to the ground.

"All right, all right," he wheezed. "Get off me."

Tansey stomped all four paws across his chest before she stepped to the side and lolled her tongue at him.

"Now that's just rude. You know what happens to

bad wolves, don't you?" His smirk hinted at a delicious tease.

She whined and crawled forward on her belly to rest her chin in his lap. Ethan stroked a hand down her neck. His fingers in her fur felt good.

He lifted his eyes to stare into the distance as the air around him grew heavy. "My folks used to end the day in this spot. No matter how many brawls he needed to break up, or what she had going on in the house, they took the time to walk up here and just be with each other. After everything that happened, he came back here only once to spread her ashes. I started coming up whenever I needed to think."

Tansey huffed a sigh and turned her attention from her mate to where he looked. She didn't need to be told the place was special. She could feel it in her bones and under her paws. The dirt thrummed with the steady heartbeat of the life Ethan breathed into his ranch.

A light breeze kicked up and blew scents of fresh grass and renewal around them. Out from under the shade of the tree, hills rolled in all directions. Mountains climbed up to the sky to the west, dark purple against the orange and pink of sunset. If she looked behind her, she knew she'd see the shapes of the big house and the smaller homes where the others in the clan lived. No matter the trouble inside those dwellings or pushing in from outside the fences, the spot itself made everything look at peace.

Ethan shared something big with her.

Tansey focused on herself and her wolf. One needed to replace the other, but she didn't exactly know how. Luckily, her wolf was in agreement and simply stepped aside.

"This is beautiful," she murmured as soon as her body became her own again. She didn't lift her head from his thigh.

Ethan grabbed a blanket from behind him and draped it over her. "I was starting to think I'd have to order you back."

That was the reason he gave for taking her to the overlook. Her wolf stayed locked inside and needed his order to appear. The transition had been hard and painful, but it bridged a gap between Tansey and that other half of herself. The calm shift back was proof, even if her limbs felt like jelly.

"I think she wanted to test you. No, that's not quite right." She didn't take her eyes off the scenery and snuggled further against Ethan. His touch soothed her. "Something close to needle and tease, but also experience. I don't know how to put it into words. She keeps flashing images of you standing over me and then jumping all around."

"Sounds like she wanted to find her place. Maybe she needed to know I was strong enough for you."

"Mmm. I think you've proven that many times over."

His phone vibrated in his pocket and he grinned down at whatever message he saw. He stroked a hand over her side, then squeezed her hip. "Put your clothes back on before I prove it again. We're needed back at the house."

Tansey grumbled and obeyed. Her wolf tumbled around her head and brushed fur against her mind. She wanted to push Ethan back to the ground and see what he would do.

Ethan flashed her a cocky, dirty smile like he knew exactly what was going on in her head, but stepped out of reach and pat his leg. "Come on, bad wolf. Do I need to lure you with dog treats?"

"I'm going to bite you," she declared.

"Counting on it," he tossed over his shoulder as he strode through the field toward home.

Tansey muttered curses under her breath and followed.

Calves nursed while their mothers continued to graze or dozed off where they stood. Ethan said they'd be integrated into the full herd in a matter of days, just as soon as they knew nothing was wrong. The close watch wouldn't end there, though. The clan would keep an eye on them as they continued to grow. The Valdana pack still lurked out there, somewhere, and no one wanted to take chances with the new lives.

Tansey slipped her hand into Ethan's. "I'm sorry Trent beat you this year."

Ethan shrugged. "It's not a real competition. It's just luck and a big party."

"And prize money."

He dipped his chin once. "That. But I have a secret weapon for that, now."

Just in time for trail rides, too. They planned to ease into letting out the extra rooms upstairs. The first couples were already booked for a handful of rides with the clan, as well as other sightseeing adventures. For her part, she had menu ideas she kept tweaking and expanding. There was a delicate balance to maintain between cookout fare and fine dining.

Instead of sneaking back into the house through the kitchen door, Ethan canted his head and led her around to the front.

Tansey sniffed the air. Something wasn't normal,

but she couldn't put her finger on it. She thought he smelled amused. Even that much was more guess than true knowledge. Her new senses were awesome when she could decipher them, which was about twenty percent of the time.

Maybe now that she and the wolf had more understanding, she'd learn fast.

She stopped dead as soon as she rounded the house and stepped into the open clearing between buildings.

A big sign proclaiming WELCOME HOME in block letters hung over the open barn doors. Someone had dragged out huge blue coolers and filled them to overflowing with ice and beer bottles. A plastic table was filled with fare from Hogshead Joint that hadn't even been removed from the takeout cartons.

Food and welcome sign aside, games of horseshoes and cornhole were set up and waiting for players. Inside one of the pens next to the barn, someone had erected a series of three barrels for what she could only assume would be their own private rodeo.

"What did you do?"

"The guys wanted to welcome you. Properly." He

leaned in and kissed her quickly. "Taking you out was a good excuse for them to get it set up."

Almost as one, the clan streamed out of the barn. They crushed her into tight hugs, and rubbed their cheeks against hers. Her wolf stirred with the motion, and inhaled each man. Earth and fur and forest were common among them, with extras that were completely individual. Jesse smelled like thick spices, while Hunter scented like fresh rain. Alex and Lorne each held tinges of worked leather, but that was where their similarities ended.

Then there was just Ethan. Her mate. Her man. The one who fought for her and with her and would make every day a curse and a blessing.

His lips hitched up on one side. "Welcome to the Black Claw clan."

The words felt like home. Seeing the ranch from Ethan's spot, finally meeting her wolf and knowing they weren't broken in their violent creation, then imprinting the others in her mind choked her with emotion. She'd been let down by the people who should have had her back, but the wild bears of Black Claw were waiting to accept her as one of them.

She didn't know what to say.

"Hey." Ethan wrapped his arms around her waist,

pulled her against him, and buried his face in the crook of her neck. "Are you sure this is what you want?"

Other questions were silently crowded into those words, but she had zero regrets for the choices taken from her or the ones she made after. Tansey twisted around so he could see the truth in her eyes as well as in her scent. "No doubts."

A low growl rumbled in his chest and his scent turned as happy as his smile. He dipped his head to lay a gentle kiss on her lips. Once, twice, then swooped in to deepen their connection.

Tansey wrapped her arms around his neck. Each brush of his tongue melted her further into his embrace. He was her rock while she flailed about in a new world. Even after she found her footing, she planned to never let go. The matching marks on their shoulders were proof of a connection that tied them together for their entire lives.

Hunter's loud whistle broke them apart. "Before you two put on a show, want to go for a run?"

Ethan cocked an eyebrow. "What do you say, wolf? Feeling too sore from earlier?"

She rolled her shoulders. The ache of her muscles was almost pleasant. Truth be told, she wanted another chance to play in her other form. "I'm up for it."

"We're in," Ethan shouted back.

One by one, the men stripped and pitched forward and bears took their places. Dark coats and light, with spots and patches, none looked exactly the same. Even their faces held a hint of their human sides. Alex looked surly. Hunter's open mouth made him as goofy as the man. Lorne and Jesse watched quietly, one standing at a distance while the other appeared almost hopeful.

Ethan stepped in front of her and hauled his shirt overhead. "Need some help?"

She swatted his hands away. "Not if we're doing this."

Within seconds, she shimmied out of her clothes and called to her wolf.

Ethan stood nearby, concern straining his face as he closely watched her shift. The time for worry had passed, and the wolf bounced in her head without any hesitation. There wasn't any battle for control or need for a stronger animal to order her into existence.

Tansey stepped aside and let the wolf take her skin. Grey and black fur slid through her pores while her muscles and bones popped and snapped to make her new shape. In seconds, the woman was replaced with the wolf.

She shook out her coat and took a cautious step forward as scents strengthened in her nose.

Five bears waited for her.

One held her heart.

Tansey lifted her snout and let loose a howl to greet the future.

ABOUT THE AUTHOR

Cecilia Lane grew up in a what most call paradise, but she insists is humid hell. She escaped the heat with weekly journeys to the library, where she learned the basics of slaying dragons, magical abilities, and grand adventures.

When it became apparent she wouldn't be able to travel the high seas with princes or party with rock star vampires, Cecilia hunkered down to create her own worlds filled with sexy people in complicated situations. She now writes with the support of her own sexy man and many interruptions from her goofy dog.

Connect with Cecilia online!
www.cecilialane.com

Shifting Destinies: Black Claw Ranch

Wrangled Fate

Spurred Fate

Breaking Fate

Wild Fate

Bucking Fate

Shifting Destinies: Shifters of Bear's Den

Forbidden Mate

Dangerous Mate

Hunted Mate

Runaway Mate

Stolen Mate

Untamed Mate

Shifting Destinies: Lion Hearts

Savage Pride

Savage Claim

Made in United States
Orlando, FL
08 February 2022

14604195R00189